"You can stay, can't you?" Lorraine whispered breathlessly as she unbuttoned Dorian's shirt.

"Yes."

"Right answer." Her hands found Dorian's breasts and reached around to unhook her bra. "I'm not sure I'd let you leave even if you wanted to." She found Dorian's mouth again, and heat rushed between Dorian's legs. Lorraine sucked on her tongue. "This way," she said, breaking the kiss and taking Dorian's hand.

The next thing Dorian knew they were in Lorraine's bedroom, kissing again and taking each other's clothes off. No one had touched Dorian this way in months. Not since Gina. Lying, cheating Gina. But Lorraine wasn't Gina, and that made all the difference.

Titles by Peggy J. Herring

Available from Bella Books

To Have
and
To Hold

PEGGY J. HERRING

Bella
BOOKS

2004

Bella Books, Inc.
P.O. Box 10543
Tallahassee, FL 32302

First published 1999 by Naiad Press

Printed in the United States of America on acid-free paper
First Edition

Editor: Lila Empson
Cover designer: Sandy Knowles

ISBN 1-59493-005-8

Acknowledgments

I'd like to thank Lisa for her input and interest in this novel. "Your" book is finally finished. Even though we met by accident, you were an immediate inspiration. And I'd like to give a special thanks to Frankie J. Jones for her constant support and input.

Chapter One

Dorian laced up her work boots and set her brown loafers on the back floorboard of the company's Geo Metro. Most of the crew were still milling around as she scanned a group near the backhoe. Dorian spotted Rusty Barnes and headed in his direction. She put her hard hat on and suppressed a smile as workers suddenly began working the moment they saw her.

Rusty waved her over and shifted the unlit, raggedy cigar to the other side of his mouth. He was a big man with a belly that hung over his belt. The seat of his pants was nothing more than a baggy reminder of where a butt should be but wasn't.

"Them neighborhood sumbitches are stealin' our dipsticks again," Rusty said in a low, rumbling voice. "We can't check the damn oil without a damn dipstick, now can we?"

"The site's been secure every night," Dorian said. She removed a pen from her starched pocket. "When's the last time the oil was checked in these things anyway?"

He eyed her with a raised bushy eyebrow and a squint. "They *better* be checkin' it every mornin'!" He tucked his clipboard under his beefy arm and looked around as someone started up the backhoe. "We got more dipsticks back at the warehouse, but I don't like kids messin' with the equipment."

Dorian was glad he let it drop. As the civil engineer for this neighborhood drainage project, Dorian was responsible for site security as well as for hundreds of other things. Even though losing dipsticks wasn't new to the crew, it had been a while since they'd had this particular problem. And from Rusty's reluctance to pursue the matter, Dorian knew that he couldn't trust his people to check the oil in their equipment every day. The dipsticks could easily have been gone for a while — misplaced or stolen somewhere else when the bulldozers were used at other sites.

"It's gonna be a scorcher today," he said. Birds were chirping, and it was already way too hot to be only seven in the morning.

"We're coming up on a water main," Dorian said. She knew the location of every underground pipe and cable within a six-block radius, and she'd taken special care that morning to inform Rusty's crew exactly where the water main was and what to watch out for. "Let's get through that first."

Dorian loved her job. She loved the sounds of the bulldozers and the jackhammers, the churning of a cement mixer and the smell of asphalt. As a civil engineer she could see results quickly, and she thrived on her accomplishments. She was responsible for helping improve neighborhoods with better storm drainage and revamped streets to serve the needs of the people. She paid taxes too `and used the taxpayer's money wisely, which most contractors despised her for. Contractors seemed to exist solely to get whatever they could out of a project, no matter whose pocket it came from.

Dorian had worked hard to get where she was. At twenty-five she had earned an engineering degree, and a few grueling exams later she'd gotten her professional engineer license. She'd been hired by a small but reputable engineering firm after her first interview, and she was one of three engineers in the office, along with two drafters and a survey crew. The Cohen Engineering staff consisted entirely of men except for Dorian and the office manager, Mia Fontaine. Dorian and the other two engineers had been hired after the boss suspected some bid rigging going on. A clean sweep of the office was made, and new blood had been added. Phil Cohen, Dorian's boss, firmly believed in letting his employees do the work. He was there if they absolutely needed him, but other than that he spent the majority of his time on the golf course.

"It's gonna be a scorcher," Rusty grumbled again. Dorian could already see sweat rings forming under his arms.

They heard some shouting directed at the backhoe operator as a small crowd gathered around the front of the huge, impressive machine. "We found that water main," someone hollered, just before light, embarrassed laughter started.

"Oh, shit," Dorian heard Rusty say as they both broke into a trot. She felt a moment of dread when she leaned over the hole and watched it fill up with water. She had hoped to prevent this, but sometimes it just couldn't be helped.

Dorian got up and dusted off her sharply creased tan pants. She and Rusty headed up the street to find the valve box to shut the water off. Neither said anything; this was all in a day's work.

Dorian checked her watch and noticed that it was just a few minutes after seven. As if on cue, irate residents up and down the block began pouring from their homes in various stages of early-morning preparedness. One man had shaving cream all over his face and shook a disposable razor at them in a threatening way. His robe flapped open, exposing light blue pajama bottoms as he yelled, "Where's my water!"

"Hey! What's goin' on?"

Total chaos erupted after that. This was one of the few aspects of Dorian's job that she didn't particularly care for. "There's been a water main break," she said calmly. "I'm sorry for any inconvenience."

"Inconvenience?" a neighborhood woman bellowed. "Inconvenience? I haven't had my *coffee* yet!"

4

Several residents headed in Dorian's direction, surrounding her with loud, booming chatter. She had to reassure them that everything that *could* be done was actually *being* done.

"You," a female voice said in a commanding, menacing tone. "You in the hard hat."

All grumbling and shouting suddenly stopped. Dorian looked up and saw a young woman in her late twenties with long, slightly disheveled early-morning blonde hair. Even in sweatpants, baggy T-shirt and socks she was attractive. Her striking blue eyes met Dorian's in a look of total disbelief.

"I've got a job interview in an hour and a half," the young woman said slowly. "When will the water be fixed?"

Dorian cleared her throat and wished she had better news for them. Dorian couldn't tell how tall the woman was because the yard sloped down to the curb and Dorian was standing in the street.

"It won't be fixed in an hour and a half," she said. "I'm sorry."

The woman's shoulders slumped, and then more chaos broke out, but Dorian held up her hands to try to calm everyone. Shouts about not having coffee, about not being able to take a shower before a doctor's appointment, about myriad other obstacles to morning necessities flew back and forth, a crescendo of angry voices building and growing as if the neighbors were trying to compete for who was in worse need of water at the moment.

"Does anyone have coffee made already?" Dorian asked the crowd. "Sharing it would be the neighborly thing to do right now."

"I've got a pot made," a man behind Dorian said. "It's a full one too. I'll share it with whoever wants some."

"And we can make more from the water in the tank on the back of our toilets," someone else commented sarcastically.

"Oh, gross!"

"I've had Harvey's coffee and it already tastes like toilet water, so what the hell?" a female voice piped in.

She heard scattered laughter at the same time that she saw Rusty hurrying back to the job site. He always made sure he stayed out of the way when his crew screwed up something.

"So let's all hitch up our jammies and go have some of Harvey's coffee," someone said. "I'm saving my toilet tank water for that one flush I'll need later."

Dorian sighed and thanked them. She wondered if the mayor's office had started getting complaints yet. Car doors slammed nearby, and tires squealed from a driveway next door, causing everyone to turn around and look. The blonde sped down the street in a Ford Taurus, no doubt heading somewhere else for water.

Dorian parked the company car in its designated space at the office and changed from her work boots to brown loafers. The other two engineers were forever teasing her about "the shoe thing," as they referred to her persistent obsession of not looking grungy when at all possible. She insisted that the "shoe thing" was a "girl thing." Tracking asphalt through the office or her apartment didn't appeal to her, and she wasn't in the least embarrassed by it. Dorian even kept a few changes of clothes in her car for those unexpected but occasional trips to the city manager's office. Dorian didn't mind getting dirty, but *staying* dirty when there were other options never made sense. Looking semipresentable at all times took very little effort, and since it made her feel better she never apologized for it.

After slipping into her relatively new loafers, she went inside the cool office building. Mia, the firm's office manager, smiled and started chuckling the moment she saw her.

"These are yours, poor baby," Mia said as she handed Dorian the huge stack of phone messages. "Be nice to me. I've already taken care of that many and then some for you. Why can't you shut off their water after they've all gone to work?" Mia teased. "Haven't I suggested that before?"

Dorian laughed and opened the door to her office. She saw the fresh bouquet of red carnations on the window sill and immediately felt better. Mia kept fresh-cut flowers in the office, adding a nice touch to the otherwise totally male environment. Mia had somehow convinced Phil, their boss, to let her set up an account with the florist next door. Phil wasn't one to part with a dollar if he didn't have to, but keeping Mia happy so the office ran smoothly was one of Phil's two priorities, the other being golf.

"Have you had lunch yet?" Mia asked from the doorway. Her long, black hair reached the middle of her back and helped emphasize her slender figure. She was a knockout, with dark eyes and a seductive smile. Her sharp wit made her the office favorite, and it was no secret that if Mia liked you, then your quality of life at Cohen Engineering was as good as it would ever be.

"No," Dorian said. "What time is it?"

"After one. I'm sending out for something. Should I get you the usual?"

"That'd be great. And thanks for the flowers."

Mia's desk, as well as the break room and the client reception area, always had fresh flowers. But whenever carnations were delivered, Mia made it a point to spruce up Dorian's office with them. Dorian was forever surprised by Mia's total recall of even the most trivial details. Her memory was phenomenal— phone numbers from year-old projects could be rattled off easily, and birthdays for every member of Phil's family didn't have to be listed anywhere. Mia ran the office like a finely tuned machine, and enjoyed reminding everyone that without her they'd all be in big trouble. Mia's point was reemphasized every September when she took her two-week vacation. Organization at Cohen Engineering all but ceased to exist during that time.

Mia returned to her desk to answer the phone while Dorian buried her face in the carnations. She allowed herself this moment to unwind before tackling the stack of phone messages. All of them seemed to be related to the water main break this morning. She sighed, knowing that the pile of messages she'd get later this afternoon would more than likely be the result of some other incident that hadn't even happened yet. Out of all the contractors that Cohen Engineering usually ended up working with, Rusty Barnes and his crew were undoubtedly the most careless. It was a challenge to bring a job in on time because of the haphazard way the crew worked. There

8

was no such thing as attention to detail or pride in one's work. Rusty was eager to finish a job no matter how shoddy or substandard the work, and, unfortunately, Cohen Engineering had little to say about it since the lowest bidding contractor almost always got the job. And if nothing else, Rusty was a genius when it came to submitting low bids and making up for it in overtime.

She sat down at her desk and shuffled through the messages. From the prefix of the phone numbers she could tell that these were irate citizens from the street with the water main break. They'd probably called the mayor's office first before being referred to the city manager's office, where, in turn, they were told to call Cohen Engineering. Dorian reached for the telephone. It was time to turn on what little charm she had left.

At eight-fifteen Friday evening Dorian was back on site to conduct a security check. She changed into work boots again and reached for her yellow hard hat in the back seat of the company car.

"Hey, lady," a young voice called. A boy and a girl, both no more than ten years old, rode up on their bicycles and stopped near the front of the car. A brown-and-white beagle followed along behind them, wagging its tail.

"You work here?" the girl asked. She had blonde hair, which came just below her shoulders, and light blue eyes. Her bicycle was a bright pink, with white streamers on the ends of the handlebars. The boy, who seemed to be a little younger, reached down to rub the dog between the ears.

"Yes, I work here," Dorian said. "Shouldn't you be home?"

"It ain't dark yet," the girl said. "We have to go in when it's dark. What's your name?"

Dorian smiled. Young girls with spunk always made her smile. Dorian had been a painfully shy child, and even now she had to make an extra effort to overcome it. Had her fourth-grade teacher not taken a special interest in her, Dorian couldn't imagine where she'd be today.

"My name's Dorian. What's yours?"

"Abby. That's Hank, my friend. And Buster," the girl said, pointing to the beagle.

"Glad to meet you, Abby. Can I ask you a question?" Dorian pushed her hard hat down snugly on her head. "Have you seen anybody around here when they shouldn't be? Playing on the bulldozers maybe?"

The two children exchanged eye contact. "Maybe," Abby said. "The mean kids down the street are over here all the time. Soon as you leave, mostly."

"How are they getting in?"

"Under the fence. It lifts right up over there."

Dorian asked them to show her, and they were eager to do so. They scrambled off their bikes and ran to the fence.

"Where do these mean kids live?" Dorian asked.

"Blue house with the mean dog," Abby said.

Dorian smiled again. "The mean kids have a mean dog?"

"They got a mean daddy, too," Hank offered. He leaned over and picked up a stick and whacked it against his handlebars to shake the dirt off. "One of

10

them kids took my bike one day and wouldn't give it back."

"You're looking for those swords, aren't you?" Abby said.

Excited, Hank asked, "Those bulldozer swords?"

Dorian suppressed a chuckle. With a little imagination, a bulldozer dipstick could look remarkably like a sword.

"Yes, I am," she said.

"The mean kids have 'em in their tree house in their backyard," Hank offered. "They've got some other stuff, too."

"It's very dangerous here," Dorian said. "This is no place for kids to be playing."

Abby reached down to pet the dog and avoided Dorian's serious look.

"It's getting dark," Dorian reminded them.

Abby and Hank crawled back on their bicycles and started peddling. Over her shoulder Abby called, "See ya later!"

Tuesday morning Dorian was in the office early, hoping to catch Phil before he left for the golf course.

"Wow. This is a surprise," Mia said. "I'm not used to seeing you here at this time of day."

"Is the boss busy?"

"He's here signing some papers," Mia said. "Go on in."

Dorian knocked on his door and found him scribbling away and then flipping through a stack of papers for the next place he was supposed to sign.

"Whatever it is, Dorian, I trust you to handle it," he said after glancing up.

She rolled her eyes and sat in one of the three chairs in front of his huge, new desk . . . "new" because he was seldom there to use it, and "huge" because Phil was the boss.

"It's Rusty," Dorian said. Whether he wanted to hear what was going on or not didn't matter at this point. She wanted Phil to hear it from her first. *I just never know when something like this will come back and bite me in the butt,* she thought.

"He offered you a bribe and you turned him down, right?" Phil said, his eyes already scanning the next document. "So what do you want me to do about it? He came in with the lowest bid so we're stuck with him, okay? That's the rule. That's the way it is. That's life in this business, Dorian. You know how it works, and you know what you have to do. I'm depending on you to bring this job in on schedule and within our estimate. You can make Rusty toe the line. You've done it before, and you'll have to do it again. Jerk his chain a little."

"He's worse than useless, Phil," she said. "A total waste of God's precious breath."

Phil laughed heartily. It was a real laugh that echoed through the office, and she knew that Mia would be after her later for a complete rerun of this entire conversation because of it.

"But, Dorian," Phil said sweetly, "Rusty speaks so highly of you."

Dorian groaned while Phil continued laughing and scribbling his name on yet another document.

"I agree that working with Rusty isn't an ideal situation," Phil said. "As contractors go, he's bringing up the rear on my list too. But he bids low and generally comes through on time. And the city manager loves that. Cheap is the name of the game. The quality of workmanship isn't a factor. And that's where *you* come in. It's *your* job to keep things running smoothly, on time, and within the regulations. How you get Rusty there in between is your problem. Make him work for it. He *hates* that." He glanced up from his papers and finally looked at her. "Handle it, Dorian. That's what I pay you for."

"Yeah, yeah, yeah," she said and stood up. Why had she expected this talk to go any differently?

"You're good at what you do," he said simply. "Trust your instincts." Phil moved his chair back, scooped the papers up in a jumbled stack and hurried to open the office door. "Mia," he called, "take these and do whatever it is you do with them."

Mia took the papers from him and slowly shook her head.

"You know where I'll be if there's an emergency," he said as he patted Dorian on the shoulder. "Otherwise, handle it."

Chapter Two

Abby was there on her bicycle every afternoon with Buster the beagle by her side. She parked her bike near Dorian's car, where she patiently watched and waited. She didn't venture close to the work site, but she was always waiting with numerous questions when Dorian was ready to leave every evening.

"You want me to help you with your boots?" Abby asked.

"No, thanks. I can do it." Dorian took off her boots and tossed them on the floorboard.

"Do you boss all those guys around?"

Dorian laughed. "Boss them? I guess you could say that."

"Girls can wear hard hats and boots too, can't they?"

"Sure they can."

"That's what I wanna do when I grow up."

"What? Boss guys around or wear boots and a hard hat?" Dorian asked. She liked this kid. Abby was curious and smart, and Dorian enjoyed the constant flow of questions from her. Just last week two bulldozer dipsticks and a canvas bag of tools mysteriously appeared outside the chained gate one morning. Apparently someone had returned a few things that had been missing for several days.

"It's getting dark," Dorian reminded her. "You and Buster better be getting home."

"Yeah, I know," Abby said as she climbed on her bike. "I just wanted to say hi before you left. I'll see you Monday."

Dorian slipped on her shoes and watched her ride away.

Friday night Dorian got home around nine-thirty. Luke, her gay neighbor, opened his apartment door and stuck his head out.

"Had dinner yet?" he asked. All she could see was a curly, black mop of hair. "I've got enough for two. Get your lovely, young dykey butt in here."

Dorian laughed and followed him inside. "My lovely, young dykey butt is dragging tonight."

"All the more reason for you to let me pamper you a little."

15

Luke was wearing cutoffs, thongs and a National-Coming-Out-Day T-shirt. A yellow measuring tape was draped around his neck.

"What exactly have you been measuring with that, young man?"

He arched an eyebrow. "I'll never tell."

Dorian noticed a sketch pad on the coffee table before her attention was drawn to a gladiator movie on the television.

"What are you watching?"

"*Spartacus*," he said. "Cedric and I are going to a toga party tomorrow night, and I'm working on our costumes. Nothing like waiting until the last minute, huh?" He brought out a bowl of popcorn and set it on the sofa between them. He handed her a gin and tonic and slipped her shoes off before putting a pair of pink bunny slippers on her feet.

"Dinner in five, hon," he said distractedly, his attention glued to the television. "Oh, my. Doesn't that Kirk Douglas have great legs?"

Dorian ignored the question, knowing Luke wasn't listening anyway. She glanced at the sketch pad again and saw several pencil drawings of togas in various stages of completion. *Did gladiators wear togas?* she wondered, turning her attention back to the movie to study costumes a bit more closely. Her stomach growled loudly and made them both laugh.

"How are things with Cedric?" she asked. Luke and Cedric had been dating for about three months. Cedric was a resident in Internal Medicine at University Hospital, and Luke was constantly complaining about his schedule.

"He's nice to look at," Luke said without taking his gaze from the television. Kirk Douglas flashed on the screen wearing a beautiful toga, and Luke snapped to life. "Oh, my. Where's the remote? That was a good toga shot."

Luke searched for the remote and backed the tape up and froze Kirk Douglas in place. After sketching furiously for several minutes, he finished with a flourish just as the timer on the oven went off. "Okay. I've got it," he said and pressed the play button to let the movie continue. "And by the way, hon, you're going with us to this toga party."

"I don't think so."

"Sure you are. I've got your toga already picked out."

Over a dinner of baked chicken and asparagus he continued to try to convince her to go.

"It'll be like visiting a nudist colony and being the only one in clothes," he warned. "After a while you'll feel weird, you know?"

Dorian held up her pink-bunny clad feet. "It doesn't get any weirder than this." He waved off her laughter and took his plate to the sink. She could sense his disappointment.

"Tomorrow's the night my office gets together for drinks," she reminded him. "If I go with you it'll only be for a little while, and no toga."

"Maybe you'll change your mind when you get there." He tossed her a triumphant smile.

Dorian laughed. "I doubt it."

The next evening Dorian insisted on taking her own car and followed Luke and Cedric to Felicia's house. Felicia was Luke's ex-wife from another lifetime. After coming out to each other they had divorced and became best friends. Dorian had met Felicia on a few occasions at Luke's place, but she and Felicia were still only acquaintances. Dorian had decided to stay at the party a polite length of time and then leave for a briefing with the city manager before meeting her coworkers at a ritzy pub called Ruffino's. Saturday night gatherings at Ruffino's helped keep the employees at Cohen Engineering in touch with each other during the summer months when Texas weather cooperated enough to keep them out of the office and working on site at various locations throughout the county. Everyone stayed busy with their own projects, so every Saturday night they met for drinks and gossip.

Several cars were already in front of Felicia's modest north side home when they arrived. Dorian parked across the street and waited as Luke got out of his car and arranged his toga in a more flattering way. Cedric seemed embarrassed and stayed in the car as long as possible.

"Still time to change your mind," Luke called across the yard, referring to Dorian's charcoal gray skirt and matching jacket. "Your toga is in the back seat here."

"No, thanks. I'm fine," she assured him.

A young toga-clad woman answered Luke's knock on the door immediately. She called over her shoulder, "Two more eunuchs. And I think they brought the Avon lady."

Avon lady, Dorian thought. She glanced down at

her white silk shirt, long gray skirt and jacket and gray boots. *I look like an Avon lady?*

"Eunuchs?" Luke said with a hand on his hip. "You bitch." He kissed the woman on the cheek and said, "We can just stop with the eunuch thing already. All systems are go with *this* plumbing, honey. You've met Cedric," he said, nudging Cedric forward a bit. "And this is my friend, Dorian, and trust me, darlin'. She's no Avon lady."

"Hi, Dorian," the young woman said, extending her hand. "I'm Victoria." She wore her hair in a long, thick braid and had an engaging smile. Her loose toga couldn't hide her round hips and large breasts. "You're not feeling festive this evening?" Victoria asked, eyeing Dorian appreciatively. "I bet you'd look even better in nothing but a sheet."

Dorian's eyes widened. Smothering a snicker, Luke grabbed her arm and led her into the living room where several women were standing around talking. A big-screen television was showing the movie *Cleopatra*, but no one seemed to be watching it.

"Don't let her get to you. She's a slut," Luke said loud enough for everyone to hear. Somewhere behind them Victoria burst out laughing.

Ruffino's, Dorian thought. *Thirty minutes max and I'm outta here.*

Felicia swooped in and gave Luke a hug. "My favorite ex-husband," she said.

"I'm your only ex-husband," Luke reminded her. "You remember Dorian, my neighbor. You two met at my Christmas party."

Felicia hugged Cedric and smiled at Dorian. "You won't be able to participate in the chariot races without a toga," Felicia informed her.

Luke patted Felicia on the arm. "She's heartbroken, I'm sure. Where's the food?"

"It's everywhere," Felicia said, waving a hand in the air.

Dorian noticed platters of grapes and cheese on the coffee table and mantel. Wine bottles and empty glasses were on the bar across the room. Never in her wildest dreams did Dorian think she would feel uncomfortable in her own clothes, but she suddenly longed to see someone dressed in something other than yards and yards of billowing white material.

"Oh, look," Luke said. "Little Romans."

Dorian was surprised to see Hank and Abby parading through the living room in togas and rope belts that gathered their costumes at the waist. Abby's radiant smile at seeing her made Dorian laugh. She wore sandals and carried a small tray of tiny, individual quiches; Hank followed along behind her in a matching toga and a pair of Fred Flintstone sneakers and carried a big bowl of chips.

"You're the hard-hat lady," Hank said, his eyes wide with surprise.

Dorian didn't know if it was one of those strange coincidences where everyone in the room suddenly stopped talking at once, or if the entire roomful of women had actually heard him and now Hank had their undivided attention.

"Avon lady, hard-hat lady . . . she answers to anything," Luke said. He leaned over toward her and asked, "Do you know this young man?"

"Sort of."

Abby smiled and set her tray down on the end of the coffee table and then hurried out of the room. As conversation picked up again, Dorian began to notice that one woman in particular was checking her out. Dorian attributed this attention to her lack of a toga.

"Come on," Luke said, tugging on Dorian's arm. "Let's go find some real food." He led the way across the hall and into the den area where more women were seated. Two additional male couples were there, and Luke began the hugging ritual and immediately became lost in conversation with an old friend. As Dorian had suspected, she didn't know anyone here but Felicia, Abby and Hank so far, and she wasn't sure she'd recognize anyone else if she did. Everyone looked pretty much alike, though the togas varied somewhat by the sashes that were worn. But basically, Dorian decided, a sheet was a sheet and there wasn't much you could do with it.

Dorian felt a tug on her jacket and turned to look down at Abby's big grin.

"You're not wearing a toga," Abby said. Her blonde hair was loosely pulled back and tied with a white ribbon. Dorian became aware of an attractive, blonde woman standing behind Abby with her hands on Abby's shoulders — late twenties, tall, blue piercing eyes. She had to be Abby's mother.

"It's you," the woman said, surprised. "You're the one who turned off my water."

Turned off your water? Dorian thought. *What are you talking about?*

Then Dorian suddenly placed the face. The water main break and the irate blonde in the sweats. The blonde who had slammed the car door and squealed down the street on her way somewhere else.

"The morning of the biggest interview of my life," the woman added.

Dorian had no idea what to say. Dealing with the public over the phone was always easier than this — the one-on-one confrontation. Dorian cleared her throat and asked, "Did you get the job?"

"Yes. No thanks to you." There was a slight smirk as the woman squeezed Abby's shoulders. "Would you join us for something to drink? You're the only thing my kid talks about these days." She nodded toward another room and slipped her hand into Abby's. Dorian followed them to the other room, where several toga-clad children were playing cards. It occurred to her for the first time that maybe not everyone in attendance was gay, but then it wasn't like Luke to waste his Saturday night at a semi-heterosexual gathering. Especially one with children.

"We haven't met officially yet," the woman said as she handed Dorian the bottled water she'd requested and gave Abby a Sprite. "I'm Lorraine Niles."

"Dorian Sadler," she said. Dorian noticed that both mother and daughter had daisies scattered in their hair and that their togas and accessories matched. Dorian met Abby's shy smile and asked, "How's Buster?"

"We gave him a bath this morning," she said. "He smelled bad." Abby handed the Sprite to Lorraine and asked, "What am I getting for my birthday?"

"I thought you wanted a pony," Lorraine said.

"Yeah, right," Abby said, rolling her eyes. "Like I'm gonna get a pony."

Hank came in and announced that they needed help with the chariot races. Abby and the other children rushed out giggling, while Felicia could be heard giving them instructions.

"That'll keep them busy for about ten minutes," Lorraine said. She and Dorian sat across from each other. Lorraine propped her head up with her hand and gave Dorian a quick once-over. "How do you know Felicia?"

"Luke, her ex-husband, is my neighbor. How about you?"

"Felicia and I went to school together." Lorraine sipped her drink and asked, "Why come to a toga party without a toga?"

"Who said I didn't have a toga?" Dorian replied.

"Then where is it?"

Dorian laughed and wondered why she was letting this woman needle her this way. And where were Luke and Cedric? How could they leave her to fend for herself in a house full of strangers?

"Let me guess," Lorraine said dryly. "Your toga's in the car."

Dorian met her skeptical gaze and took a sip of her bottled water.

"You're probably one of those people who go to Tupperware parties and don't buy anything," Lorraine said.

"Is all this hostility stemming from the water main break that wasn't my fault?"

"Hostility?" Lorraine said, surprised. "I'm not hostile at all. By the way, that's a very nice jacket you're wearing." She studied it for a moment and then looked away. "You're not dressed like a lesbian."

Dorian was once again speechless, but finally managed to ask, "And what does a lesbian dress like?"

"We wear togas to toga parties, for one thing."

Their mutual laughter relaxed Dorian a bit.

"So how long have you been in construction?" Lorraine asked.

"About four years. I'm actually a civil engineer."

"You're kidding. Really?" Lorraine seemed to look at her more closely then. "I thought you were a construction worker. Driving a steamroller or bulldozer or something constructionish. You know. The hard hat and all. Wow. A civil engineer."

"I design the things that the construction workers make," Dorian said. "And I make sure they're doing it right."

Lorraine crossed her legs and began swinging a sandled foot. "How interesting. Where'd you go to school?"

"MIT."

Lorraine smiled and nodded her blonde head. "Very good."

A steamroller operator, Dorian thought. *First I'm mistaken for the Avon lady and then someone thinks I'm a construction worker.* She looked down at her gray skirt and jacket and wondered briefly what Avon ladies actually wore these days.

An announcement requested everyone's presence in the backyard. A parade of wine-sipping toga wearers ambled down the hallway toward the festivities. Dorian saw this as the perfect time to leave, but Luke was suddenly at her elbow ushering her outside.

"Five," he whispered. "Count 'em —*five* women have asked me about you already."

She looked at him as though he were crazy. She wasn't quite sure whether to believe him or not.

"The one on the left over there," he whispered, "the one with the palm leaf fanning Felicia."

"What about her?"

"Stay away from that one," he said. "She's like a praying mantis. She eats her mate when she's through with her."

"Hmm," Dorian said. "Sounds interesting, but I'm not into mating. Thanks." She watched for a moment as the children lined up bright red wagons on the lush grass. Lorraine was helping Abby reattach a paper flower to the side. Lorraine looked up, met Dorian's lingering gaze, and smiled before returning her attention to replacing the flower on the wagon.

"What are you drinking?" Luke asked, his eyes clearly showing disgust at the bottle of water she was holding.

Dorian laughed and squeezed his arm. "I need to get going. The city manager is expecting me. His schedule's worse than mine, and this is the only time he could see me."

Luke walked her to her car. "All those women in there," he said. "Why won't you let me fix you up with one of them?"

Dorian felt a dull ache at the memory of Gina and their yearlong relationship. Gina was a friend of a co-worker of Luke's and he had introduced them at a Christmas party two years ago. Neither Luke nor Dorian knew that Gina was married until she announced after several months that she not only had a husband but that she was also pregnant. Dorian was devastated. She had thrown up for three days and cried for a week. Even though Gina claimed to be in love with her, she wouldn't leave her husband.

Dorian looked at Luke in the glow from the street-light and said, "I can get my own dates, thank you very much."

He chuckled and gave her a hug. "Your toga will be in the car if you change your mind later."

"Not likely, but thanks."

Chapter Three

Ruffino's hosted its usual Saturday night crowd, but Cohen Engineering had a nice big table in the back with eight people around it. Dorian was relieved to see that Mia, as well as the wives of the two other engineers and the wife of a surveyor, had already arrived. The wives helped make the gathering less of an office thing and more of a social event.

"Look who's here," Mia said and pulled out an empty chair beside her.

"I think it's Dorian's turn to buy a round of drinks," Charlie said. Charlie Rosen and Will Garcia were the other two engineers in the office, besides their boss, Phil Cohen. Phil had hired Will and Charlie the same day he had hired Dorian.

They exchanged field stories, told jokes and tried to get Mia to share some dirt on Phil Cohen, but Mia would only smile and shake her head. She would tell them nothing, and everyone knew it, but it was a ritual they went through anyway.

Mia sipped her wine and twirled the glass at the stem. She wore a white, one-piece jumpsuit that clung to her body in all the right places. Dorian couldn't remember ever seeing her in that outfit before. Mia pushed her long, black hair away from her face, and her dark, friendly eyes danced with mischief. She was stunning, and had what the men in the office referred to as the Mia Mystique — a phenomenon that everyone took for granted now. Mia could answer a question before it was completely asked, and she knew where things were when they'd been misplaced for days. Bailey, one of the surveyors, had taken to calling her Radar.

"Dorian made him laugh one morning this week," Mia said, addressing the others at the table. "A *loud* laugh."

"Phil never laughs," Charlie noted.

"My point exactly," Mia said.

All eyes were now on Dorian, and she could feel the heat rising in her face. *I'm blushing, damn it. Now I'll never hear the end of this.*

"He likes golf jokes," Mia said. She cocked her head and smiled playfully at Dorian. "Did you tell him a golf joke?"

Dorian shrugged. "I don't remember what we were talking about then. Sorry. But it wasn't a golf joke."

From there Will remembered a golf joke and then they were off telling jokes again. Someone ordered another round of drinks, and a while later the partyers started checking their watches. Charlie and Rose were the first to leave, and then Will and his wife followed soon after. Dan, Lawrence, and Bailey were off to check out a new country bar at one of the malls.

"I think you two should come with us," Dan said. He was a drafter in his late twenties and sported a crew cut that needed a little maintenance. He was single, and partying stayed on his mind a lot. Dan was famous for his Monday-morning hangovers.

Dorian and Mia declined the invitation, and the next thing Dorian knew she and Mia were the only ones left at the table.

"Let's move to a booth," Dorian said. They ordered decaf coffee, and it occurred to Dorian as she watched Mia stir cream into her cup that she knew very little about this woman. There was never a mention of children, a husband or a boyfriend, and there were no pictures on her desk to indicate what her family situation might be. Mia was funny and smart, and ran the office flawlessly during Phil's absence. Dorian wouldn't be surprised to learn that Mia was the highest-paid person on staff. She was loyal to Phil and seemed happy at her job. Dorian certainly knew how fortunate they were to have her there for them every day.

Mia set the spoon on the table and took a sip. "Why can't they make a good cup of decaf?" She set the cup back down and moved it away from her. "Brown water," she said. "That's not coffee."

Dorian took a cautious sip and agreed. She settled comfortably into the booth and pulled her cup closer.

"Where do you expect to be in five years?" Mia asked suddenly. She shifted, and Dorian noticed how enticingly low the zipper was on Mia's jumpsuit. Dorian took a deep breath and tried to concentrate on answering the question.

"Five years," Dorian said thoughtfully. "Hmmm. I don't know. I like what I'm doing. I can easily see myself in the same job for quite a while."

"The city would snatch you up in a heartbeat," Mia said. "Phil plays golf with the city manager, and Hector is always telling him what a great job you're doing. Besides, none of the city's engineers are women, and that doesn't look good."

"There's too much politics when you work for the city," Dorian said. "I'm happy where I am right now. Even if it means having to work with Rusty Barnes."

Mia smiled and swept her hair away from her face in one smooth, easy motion. "Rusty 'No-Butt' Barnes," she said with a laugh.

Dorian shrugged. "Phil's been good to me. I think we've surprised each other."

Mia nodded. "I remember the day you interviewed. He was very impressed with you."

Dorian remembered that day as well. She had felt good about the interview and had immediately liked Phil Cohen and his work ethic. Money wasn't everything to Phil. He took pride in his work and didn't mind paying his people what they were worth.

"And he's still impressed with you," Mia said. "You're not a whiner, and you can make a decision on your own. Do you have any idea how often Charlie and Will are in his office?"

Dorian laughed away her embarrassment at the compliment. "I take it we have whiners."

"Yes, Dorian, we have whiners." Mia reached into her small, black purse and placed some bills on the table. "And let me also add that Phil isn't the only one who's impressed with you."

Dorian sat in shocked silence as Mia winked at her. "Good night, Dorian. I'll see you on Monday."

Dorian drove home feeling strangely elated. It had been an unusual evening, but one that had left an impression on her. Much later, off and on during the night as she tossed and turned in bed, Dorian dreamed about white togas and zippers on black leather. She woke up tired the next morning and promised herself she'd do absolutely nothing all day.

Fresh from a shower on Sunday morning, Dorian emerged in shorts and a T-shirt, but her hair was still wet and shaggy when Luke came over to get her for breakfast. Once they were in his apartment, Dorian offered to set the table and nearly swooned at the smell of banana-flavored decaf coffee and warm blueberry muffins.

"You caused quite a stir at the party last night," he said. Luke was acting a bit campy and insisted that she use the china for their muffins. He flitted back and forth between the kitchen and dining room, on each trip carrying in something else they needed . . . first the butter then the cream cheese. On another trip he brought the coffee in a carafe and then went back for sugar.

"Lorraine was sooo embarrassed about mistaking

you for a construction worker, honey," he said. "She sends her apologies again."

"She talked to you about me?" Dorian asked, surprised by his comment.

"You were the main topic of conversation most of the night," Luke said emphatically. "There were five shes grilling me about you, including the slut who answered the door. But let's not count her."

"You're lying."

With thin fingers spread, he placed his hand over his heart as if in distress. "Like I've got nothing better to do than fabricate admirers for you."

"What did they want to know?" Dorian asked with a crinkled brow. After a moment she shook her head as if coming to her senses. "You're lying," she decided without giving it another thought.

Luke buttered a muffin with quick exaggerated sweeps of his knife. "Suit yourself. The redhead offered to bear my children for your phone number though."

Dorian hooted.

"And the slut at the door —"

"Why do you keep calling her that?" Dorian asked, irritated by the word.

"I've seen her in action on a dance floor."

Dorian filled their cups and added cream to her coffee. She had been told on numerous occasions how attractive she was, but she had never taken the compliments seriously. Whatever it was that women saw in her was a complete mystery to her. The nature of Dorian's work kept her in shape, but she thought of herself as about three inches too tall and a bit too plain to be considered anything more than vaguely interesting. Her shoulder-length light brown hair was her best asset, even though she had once been told that she had a "camera-perfect" smile. Her father had paid big bucks for that smile, and Dorian now appreciated every trip her mother had made with her to the orthodontist. Luke, however, had piqued her curiosity. What if he wasn't lying after all?

"Did someone really ask about me?" she said, sipping her coffee and trying to sound uninterested.

"Yes, someone really asked about you. Five," he said. "Count 'em. Five someones." Luke took a dainty bite of muffin before continuing. "But only two were suitable. Lorraine actually had Felicia-My-Ex ask me a few things. She wasn't as obvious as the others."

"Five," Dorian repeated in disbelief, and then she laughed again, refusing to fall for it. "You're lying."

Luke set his knife down to a clatter of china. "Suit yourself. No wonder you're still single. Is this the way you are when women come on to you?"

"Women don't *come on* to me."

Luke rolled his eyes. "Oh, puleeze. Don't give me that. I've *seen* them!"

"When?" Dorian challenged. "The slut at the door last night?" She could feel her face getting red again. "I can't believe I said that," she mumbled as she pulled a muffin apart.

Luke snickered and then looked at her thoughtfully for a moment. "You really don't see it, do you?"

"Let's talk about something else," Dorian suggested, embarrassed by the sudden change in Luke's intensity.

"And women *do* come on to you."

"I don't think so."

"Now I remember why you needed my help before."

Dorian's look was meant to stop him cold, which it did. Luke squirmed a little and then shrugged. Gina and that whole twelve-month fiasco was still a touchy subject between them.

"I don't need your help finding women," she said.

"No, of course not. Your phone's constantly ringing and you've got them lined up in the hallway waiting for a chance to —"

"I don't need your help finding women," she said a bit louder this time.

He snatched another muffin from the basket and began vigorously spreading cream cheese on it. "I fuck up once, Dorian, *once*, and you hold it against me forever. I swear to God I didn't know she was married."

"I believe you. Now let's talk about something else." Dorian's appetite was gone. Gina still had that effect on her.

"We could watch *Spartacus*," Luke suggested. "I need to take it back tomorrow. I borrowed it from a friend. I was so busy making costumes I never really got to see any of it."

Dorian looked at him expectantly, as if hoping he had another idea about how to spend a Sunday afternoon. She finished her coffee and set the cup down easily. "*Spartacus*," she said and then shook her head. "Luke, my friend. We both need to get a life."

The drainage project moved along nicely. Construction was now two blocks away from where the project had started, but the neighborhood kids kept a steady vigil on their progress. Some members of Rusty's crew were forever running the kids off, but Dorian was a firm believer that fewer things would come up tampered with or missing if you were friendly with the neighborhood children.

Abby was there every afternoon, waiting on her pink bicycle, always eager for Dorian's attention. She had questions to ask and seemed truly interested in what would happen next on the site. They usually spent at least five minutes together while Dorian changed out of her boots and into real shoes, and lately when their conversations had centered on engineering in particular, Dorian had been even slower in leaving.

"Good grades are a must if you want to be an engineer," Dorian said. "And especially math. Do you like math?"

"Sure," Abby said with a shrug. "It's my favorite subject. Was it yours too?"

"Yes, it was. Just keep at it." Dorian stood up and set her gunky boots in the floor of the back seat, signaling that their talk was over.

"Tomorrow's my birthday," Abby said. "Can you come to my house?"

Hoping to avoid the direction the conversation was taking, Dorian asked how old she would be. "Ten. Rainey said I could have two friends over for cake and stuff. Please, please, please. Will you come?"

"I don't know," Dorian said. "I have other work I have to do when I leave here."

"You wouldn't have to stay real long. And you don't have to get me a present or anything," Abby said. The disappointment on her young face made Dorian momentarily feel awful.

"Please?" Abby said again. "I'm having a party on Saturday, but my birthday's really tomorrow. Please? Will you come?"

Dorian smiled at her persistence but didn't want to promise anything. "We'll see."

Chapter Four

The next morning Dorian called the office to ask Mia for a favor. "The smallest one you can find," she said. "And new. It needs to be new."

"Any idea when you'll be in today?" Mia asked.

Dorian stuck a finger in her ear as a backhoe roared past her. "I'm shooting for three unless things start falling apart here. Just see what you can do. And I really appreciate this."

"No problem," Mia said. "See you at three, but call first. I might not be able to find one."

Dorian tucked the small phone back in her pocket.

She knew absolutely *nothing* about kids, but had an idea what Abby would like. Shopping for her numerous nieces and nephews consisted of calling a sister-in-law for specific details on what the kids wanted. So having to come up with an idea on her own now was close to traumatic.

It was already well after three when Dorian noticed the time. She called the office to see if Mia had been able to get what she wanted.

"Brand-new," Mia said. "You'll be pleased. I'm wrapping it for you as we speak."

"Really? You found one? I'm on my way."

At the office, Mia had the present wrapped in colorful Little Mermaid paper with a bright yellow bow. She slid a pen and a card over and told her to sign it.

"This is great," Dorian said with relief. "A card and everything," she said as she signed the card and tucked the flap in on the envelope. Before leaving with the present, Dorian placed a crisp twenty-dollar bill discreetly on the desk. "Here. Take this and don't argue. Wrapping paper and birthday cards don't grow on trees."

Mia looked at the money and then at Dorian with an arched eyebrow. "And where, pray tell, *does* wrapping paper and such come from, if not from trees?"

"You know what I mean."

"Keep your money. I had all this here already. The card included."

"Then consider it a donation to the coffee fund or something," Dorian said as she turned the present and admired the professional-looking wrapping job. "Jesus, I hope this is a good idea."

"It's a great idea," Mia said seriously. And then she added, "Give me complete details tomorrow."

Rusty's ears began to get red, and then he took the ratty, unlit cigar out of his mouth and jabbed it at Dorian as he made his point. No, he wasn't paying his crew overtime out of his pocket to fix a few driveways. The driveways were thirty years old already, and his backhoe hadn't hurt them any.

"It's concrete, goddamn it!" he roared. "Them driveways didn't look much better before we got here."

"I'm not going to argue about this, Rusty," Dorian said calmly. "If you don't fix them by Friday afternoon, I'm holding up the vouchers. No fix — no pay. Am I making myself clear?"

His face was completely red now. If he had been a cartoon character, steam would have spewed from his ears. He stuffed the cigar back in his mouth and stomped off toward his truck. Dorian made a note to check how many driveways and curbs had been damaged during the sewer-pipe break earlier in the day.

Dorian changed out of her boots and slipped into her loafers. The festively decorated present on the seat caught her eye and reminded her that she needed to drop it off. Abby had given her the address the day before, and even though Dorian had a good idea where Abby lived, she wasn't sure which house Lorraine had stormed back to the morning of the water main break. After a while, most of the houses in this neighborhood began to look the same.

Rusty and his crew had ruined several curbs

during their ten-minute backhoe rodeo earlier that morning, and as she got in the car, Dorian thought about the stack of phone messages that were sure to be awaiting her at the office. *Some things never change,* she thought. She wondered if Rusty paid his backhoe operators extra just to make her life miserable.

She found Abby's house easily and ran her fingers through her thick, curly hair, but she couldn't tell any difference in the way it looked in the rearview mirror. With the present tucked under her arm, Dorian stepped up on the porch and knocked on the door. A few seconds later Lorraine answered and stood there with a surprised expression. Abby squeezed past her with a huge grin.

"You came!"

Lorraine held the door open and moved out of the way, the surprise on her face now a playful smirk.

"Happy birthday," Dorian said, handing the present to Abby.

"Oh, wow. Thanks." Paper went flying right away, and then Dorian noticed Hank beside Abby helping her hold the box while she struggled with the stubborn bow.

"I didn't expect to see you here," Lorraine said.

"Why? Abby and I talk almost every day," Dorian said. "She's very inquisitive."

Lorraine laughed. "Yes. That she is."

The box and the chaos surrounding its undoing drew their attention. Abby pulled the small yellow hard hat out of the tissue paper and, with a squeal, put it on her head.

"It's just like yours, ain't it?" Abby said. "Oh, wow! Look, Rainey! She got me a hard hat just like hers!"

"That one's a little cleaner than mine, I think," Dorian said. For the first time all day she felt as though she'd selected the right gift. Once during the afternoon she'd decided to forget the whole thing, but now she was glad she hadn't.

"You're a hit," Lorraine said. She reached over and thumped the top of Abby's hat a few times and shook her head and laughed.

"We're having hot dogs and Jell-O as soon as Uncle Ethan gets here," Abby said. "And cake, too, later."

"I need to get going," Dorian said. She knew what was waiting for her at the office. Rusty's crew and their disregard for other people's property would cause her countless hours of extra work.

To Dorian's surprise, Lorraine seemed almost as disappointed as Abby did at the announcement that she couldn't stay. Just then the door opened and a very handsome man came in. He was in his early thirties with short, neatly combed blond hair. This had to be Uncle Ethan, Dorian decided. There was a strong resemblance between Lorraine, Ethan and Abby. Introductions were made, and Dorian and Ethan shook hands.

"Let's eat," Lorraine said. She turned to Dorian and said, "Are you sure you can't stay for hot dogs and orange Jell-O? It's Abby's favorite, and it's her birthday. We'd really like for you to join us."

The invitation was sincere, and Dorian was surprised to find herself actually wanting to stay. "These hot dogs aren't *in* the Jell-O, are they?" Dorian inquired.

"Oh, yuck," Abby said. "They better *not* be!"

And so it went. Hot dogs were prepared with every condiment imaginable lined up on the table. And a small bowl of orange Jell-O was put beside each place setting. Dorian was surprised at how good that first hot dog tasted. Lorraine kept their glasses full of fresh lemonade, and Dorian noticed the cake with unlit candles on the counter, waiting for attention.

"And we get coffee later, right?" Abby asked. She still had her hard hat on, which complemented the mustard smudge on her cheek.

"Yes," Lorraine said. "You can have coffee with your cake later." She went on to explain to Dorian and Ethan that the coffee Abby would be getting was decaf and would be more like a coffee-flavored milkshake by the time Abby got ready to drink it.

Lorraine asked about the project Dorian was currently working on and told her that Abby was keeping her posted on its progress every day.

"She wanted a telescope for her birthday because she saw you looking through one several weeks ago," Lorraine said.

"A telescope?" Dorian said, and then it occurred to her what Abby might have seen. "Maybe she saw me with a transit. A small telescope-like thing that surveyors use." She glanced over at Abby, who was attempting to flick a glob of Jell-O at Hank. She looked adorable in the hard hat, her blonde hair barely touching her shoulders and her bangs a bit too long. Dorian was very aware of what little effort it really took to be a positive influence on a child's life. She made a promise to herself to make a point of being more attentive to Abby while she worked in the area.

"You haven't even asked about *my* present yet," Ethan said a while later.

Abby's eyes lit up as she started in on her second helping of orange Jell-O. "Where is it?"

"Front seat of my car."

Abby and Hank scrambled out of their chairs and raced to the door. Lorraine took another bite of Jell-O and then pointed her spoon at her brother as if to issue a warning, but then thought better of it. The front door slammed again, and Abby came rushing in with her arms full.

"Bazookas! I got water bazookas for my birthday!" She held a huge plastic water gun up with one hand and pushed the hard hat down firmly on her head with the other. "There's four, Rainey. Can we play with 'em now? Can we?"

"The back yard," Lorraine said with a nod.

Ethan and the two children chose their weapons and hurried out the back door, leaving Dorian and Lorraine alone at the table. Lorraine picked up the remaining huge water gun and took it to the kitchen where she began filling it with water at the sink. Dorian followed her to the kitchen and leaned against the doorjamb and watched.

Lorraine was an attractive woman. Late twenties, long blonde hair and fine Norwegian features. In shorts, a T-shirt and sneakers, her runner's body had a much nicer shape than the toga had revealed weeks ago.

"Let's go out on the back porch," Lorraine said. Once outside she leaned the loaded water gun against the house and then sat down on the top step.

"Abby idolizes you," Lorraine said, wrapping her arms around her knees. "She talks about you constantly. Thanks for staying. I know it means a lot to her."

A little embarrassed by her earlier plans to just drop the gift off and head for the office, Dorian said quietly, "My pleasure."

Their attention was drawn back to the yard where the three drenched water-gun warriors were playfully fighting over the hose to reload their weapons. Ethan whispered something to the children and nodded toward the porch.

"Don't even think about it," Lorraine warned.

The three in the yard cackled outrageously before continuing to fill their weapons.

"One more round," Lorraine called. "We've still got cake to eat."

Bazookas were reloaded, and a new battle broke out with drenched, squealing participants thoroughly enjoying themselves.

"Would you be out there with them if I weren't here?" Dorian asked.

Lorraine leaned her head back and chuckled but didn't answer. Her blonde hair cascaded down past her shoulders.

"You would, wouldn't you?" Dorian said. She casually reached for the remaining water gun propped against the house and then pointed it at her.

"Should I put my hands up?" Lorraine asked dryly.

"That won't be necessary."

"So help me. If you get me wet..."

"Stand up," Dorian said. They both got up and Dorian urged her with the end of the bazooka. "Now here," she said. "Take this and go out there and join them."

"No, thanks," Lorraine said. "You'll need it more than I will." She jumped from the porch and grabbed the water hose that was still running full force in the yard. She turned and sprayed a fierce stream that caught Dorian in the left shoulder first and within two seconds had soaked her from head to toe. Lorraine then made a sweep of the yard with the hose, hitting the other three as well. Dorian stood on the porch, blinking in astonishment and gasping as her wet cold clothes touched previously warm skin.

Lorraine spun back around and got Dorian again, shouting, "This is for shutting off my water before the biggest interview of my life!"

The three warriors in the yard turned their water guns on Lorraine, causing her to turn from Dorian to defend herself.

Dorian took advantage of this distraction and gracefully jumped down from the porch and came up behind her as Lorraine ruthlessly sprayed her squealing daughter and brother into submission. Dorian dropped the water gun and grabbed the hose away from Lorraine with one smooth move. She stuffed the hose down the back of Lorraine's pants. Lorraine swirled around with the same surprised, wild expression Dorian imagined she herself had earlier. Lorraine gasped and sucked at air as she tried desperately to fumble for the hose, but Dorian held it firmly in place as a steady stream of cold water flowed down her body.

"And that's for calling me a construction worker," Dorian said simply.

Chapter Five

An hour later, everyone was in dry clothes and gathered around the table finishing cake and coffee. They were all still laughing about the water-gun fight. Their clothes were tumbling in the dryer in the laundry room. Lorraine had loaned Dorian and Ethan sweatshirts, running shorts and socks to wear while waiting.

"I'm sorry about your shoes," Lorraine said sheepishly. "I didn't think." Everyone looked in the corner where Dorian's waterlogged new loafers sat.

With an impish grin Lorraine suggested, "We could pop them in the microwave."

"Uh . . . that won't be necessary."

Lorraine's smirk turned into a slow, easy smile as they looked at each other. Dorian was attracted to her, and she sensed that Lorraine was feeling the same. But Dorian had been wrong before, and she never trusted her instincts with women. Rather than pursue that line of thought, she turned her attention to Abby and asked what else she had gotten for her birthday.

"A telescope," Abby said. "But it's still in the box. Uncle Ethan's supposed to put it together for me."

"You'd think a civil engineer could do it faster," Ethan said. "I'm not very mechanical."

Dorian, Abby and Hank spent the next several minutes assembling the telescope and lining up the sight. Dorian explained which planets were visible and warned Abby and Hank not to use the telescope to look at the sun.

"And no spying on the neighbors," Lorraine said, coming up behind them. The dryer buzzed annoyingly, and she left to tend to it. Ethan carried the telescope out on the front porch to check out the night sky with the children. Dorian followed Lorraine to the laundry room, running her fingers through her semidamp hair along the way. Lorraine got their clothes out and began folding them neatly into separate stacks.

"It's been a long time since I've had another woman in my shorts," Lorraine said with that teasing smirk.

Dorian glanced down at her borrowed outfit and knew her face was turning a glaring shade of red. She laughed nervously before saying, "It's been a while since I've *been* in another woman's shorts."

Lorraine chuckled and handed over Dorian's warm, dry clothes. "I'm really sorry about your shoes," she said again. "I've got an extra pair you can borrow to drive home in."

Dorian explained that it wasn't necessary. She had work boots in the car she could use. "I had fun tonight," Dorian said. "Thanks for inviting me."

"It's been our pleasure."

Dorian took her clothes into the bathroom and changed. It was too late to go to the office and get anything done there. She'd have to go in early and see what needed to be taken care of. She decided to make a security check at the job site before going home.

She found everyone on the front porch hovering around the telescope. Abby asked Dorian if she could come to her big birthday party on Saturday.

"We'd love to have you," Lorraine said. "You won't get wet, I promise. Cake, ice cream, piñata. Just the usual."

"What time and where?" Dorian asked. She was very aware that the thought of seeing the mother again made this birthday thing quite appealing.

"At one. Here," Lorraine said, thrusting an invitation in her hand. "Twelve ten-year-olds. I need to warn you about that part."

"I'll see what I can do," Dorian said.

Abby came over and hugged Dorian, and she was once again glad she had stayed. "Thanks for the hard hat, Dorian. I really like it."

"You're welcome. Happy birthday."

As Dorian drove home, she thought about the amused, interested looks that Lorraine had given her off and on during the evening. It was definitely more interesting to think about than broken water pipes, shoddy workmanship and Rusty Barnes and his chewed-up cigars.

Monday afternoon when Dorian arrived at the job site Abby was waiting for her. She was riding her bike and wearing her hard hat, but her expression wasn't a friendly one.

"You didn't come to my party Saturday."

"I'm sorry," Dorian said. "I ended up having to work and didn't have your phone number with me. I spent the whole weekend on the roof of the Alamodome, which wasn't exactly my favorite place to be. So tell me about the party. How was it? Did you get lots of presents?"

"Yeah."

"What all did you do?" Dorian prompted.

"Birthday stuff."

"Hmm. How long are you going to stay mad at me?"

Abby's pout turned into a weak smile. "I don't know."

A car pulled up beside them, and Lorraine rolled down her window. "You're not supposed to be over this far," she said to Abby. "You know the rules."

"Rules, rules, rules," Abby grumbled as she scuffed the toe of her shoe in the grass.

Lorraine got out of the car. She looked great in tight Levi's and a work shirt with the sleeves rolled up. She unlocked the trunk and put Abby's bicycle in it.

"We missed you on Saturday," Lorraine said. "She waited for you all day."

"I'm sorry. Something came up."

"She had to fix the Alamodome," Abby said proudly. "If you come over later I won't be mad anymore. We can play with my water guns again."

With a chuckle, Lorraine said, "You're a real charmer, Abby dearest. Now we'll probably never see her again."

Dorian shrugged. "A little water never hurt anybody. Maybe I'll see you later then."

"Don't say it if you don't mean it," Lorraine said seriously. "Abby likes you. This is important to her."

"I know. I'll be over later."

Dorian got back to the office about twenty minutes before Mia was ready to close up. Mia handed over the stack of messages and told her that her brother had called.

"Joseph?" Dorian asked, even though she had a good idea which brother it was. Joseph had been trying to get her to visit him at the coast before the funding ran out on his latest project. Joseph and his wife were marine engineers working with the Texas Historical Commission.

"Yes," Mia confirmed. "It was Joseph. He always tells me such interesting things about you."

Dorian cringed. "Don't believe everything you hear."

"I don't," Mia said. "Trust me. How's it going with Rusty?"

"The usual. Contractors are the lowest life form there is."

"My, my, Ms. Sadler," Mia said with a laugh as Dorian headed for her office.

A while later Mia came to Dorian's door. "I'm leaving. Don't work too late."

"Never been accused of that."

When Mia made no further attempt to leave, Dorian looked up from her notes.

"How are you really?" Mia asked.

"I'm fine. Why?"

Mia tossed long black hair off her shoulder. "No reason. Just checking."

Dorian smiled. "Well, thanks for checking. And thanks for keeping the flowers in here." She nodded toward the window sill where the vase of red carnations stood. "They always cheer me up no matter what kind of day I've had."

Mia moved away from the door. "Don't stay too late. I'll see you tomorrow."

It was eight-thirty by the time Dorian returned to the job site for a security check. It was later still when she drove by Lorraine and Abby's house. The lights were still on.

"We'd given up on you," Lorraine said. "Come in."

"I'm sorry it's so late."

Abby came in wearing pajamas and her hard hat. She wanted to show Dorian her room and took her by the hand and led the way. A small television and a VCR were on a stand near the door with several Disney movies neatly stacked beside them. The four huge water guns took up a large portion of another wall. Dr. Seuss and an old set of Nancy Drew mysteries were in a small bookcase. A few dirty clothes were on the floor near a hamper, but overall the room was orderly.

Dorian examined a picture on the nightstand by Abby's bed. It was a young woman with long, dark hair. She was pretty and had dimples that added character to her face. Dorian set the picture down and glanced around the room again.

"That's a picture of my real mom," Abby said. She went on to explain that her mother had died a long time ago.

"She was very pretty," Dorian said. "You have her eyes."

Abby smiled. "That's what Rainey says. She tells me stories about her."

"Which story's your favorite?" Dorian asked. She was confused by this new information since Lorraine and Abby looked so much alike, but Dorian didn't ask her any questions.

"The elephant-snot story." Abby giggled.

"Oh," Dorian said, curling up her nose.

"Last week it was the dill-pickle-and-peanut-butter story," Lorraine said from the doorway. She came into the room and motioned toward the bed. "Under the covers, kiddo. It's that time."

Abby took her hard hat off and carefully set it on the dresser. She gave Dorian a hug and then gave one to Lorraine.

"Next time you come over we'll play with my water guns, okay?" Abby said.

"Hmm," was Dorian's only response as she went back to the living room. It was getting late, but she wasn't ready to leave yet. She spotted more pictures on the mantel and studied them closely.

"I'm not Abby's mother," Lorraine said as she came into the room. "Tess died of complications a few hours after Abby was born."

Dorian didn't know what to say. They went to the sofa and sat a reasonable distance apart. Lorraine seemed comfortable, so Dorian just listened and let her talk.

"I was expecting to bring my lover and our daughter home from the hospital," she said quietly. "Instead I found myself making funeral arrangements and tending to a newborn. Having Abby was the only thing that got me through it." Lorraine smiled sadly and crossed her arms over her chest. "And she's still getting me through it." She ran her hands briskly along her arms and shook her head as if to clear it. "Will you have a glass of wine with me?"

"Sure." Dorian followed her to the kitchen, still at a loss for words.

"Tess and I were deliriously happy together for three years. We had dreams of a mortgage, a two-car garage and, eventually, a baby. Life's full of surprises. Sometimes it's not fair." She handed Dorian a glass of wine. "So tell me something about you. All I know is that you're single, you're a civil engineer and my kid's got this huge crush on you."

Dorian blushed again. "It's the hard hat," she said. They moved back to the living room, Dorian in a chair and Lorraine on the sofa.

"Every day she comes home and tells me what you two have talked about," Lorraine said. "Like the telescope. She just had to have one. At this point I'm just glad you don't ride a motorcycle and have various body parts pierced. She'd probably want that next."

"And what makes you think I'm not pierced anywhere?" Dorian asked.

Lorraine laughed. "You wear loafers, for crissakes. You don't strike me as the pierced type. Sorry."

"Hmm. I'm not sure that's a compliment."

With the help of the wine, Dorian eventually got the courage to ask her if she'd be interested in a little adventure. She went on the explain that she had to go out of town on Saturday to see her brother and his wife.

"They're working on a project at Matagorda Bay on the coast. My brother's been after me to visit and see what he's been doing down there. It should be fun if you're at all interested in old shipwrecks."

"You mean the *LaBelle* excavation? The one they've built the cofferdam around?"

Dorian blinked several times and was momentarily speechless. "You've heard about it?"

"I've been following it in the paper," Lorraine said. "What does your brother have to do with it? I thought only archaeologists were allowed on the site."

"Plus marine engineers and a host of volunteers. My brother and sister-in-law built the cofferdam that surrounds the wreck. He's been trying to get me down there for months so he can show it off, but I haven't had time to go. And now that the project's close to the end, I need to quit procrastinating and just do it."

"I can't believe this!" Lorraine said excitedly. "Tess and I are big Texas history buffs and love talking and reading about this shipwreck."

"Then you'll go?" Dorian asked. For some reason

this surprised her. "It'll be a great experience for Abby too. A boat ride out to the site, seeing all the artifacts they've uncovered and the cofferdam."

"I've seen pictures in the paper," Lorraine said. "This is really exciting."

Dorian happened to see what time it was as she set her glass down on the table. "Hey, I'd better get going. I could yak about this all night." She got up and pulled her keys out of her pocket.

"Why don't you come by for dinner tomorrow and I can tell you what led up to the shipwreck?" Lorraine said. "It's spaghetti night. Nothing fancy." She walked with her outside. "I have the feeling you're more interested in the engineering aspects of this trip anyway, and I think you'll enjoy the whole thing much more if you're familiar with the historical significance of this find."

"Hmm. What exactly do you have in mind?" Dorian asked. "Sounds like homework."

Lorraine laughed. "Not at all. So can we expect you for dinner? We can talk more about your homework then."

On the way home Dorian felt rejuvenated and giddy. The thought of spending more time with Lorraine and Abby was an adventure in its own right. Seeing her brother and a shipwreck would be an added bonus.

Dorian had a bad day at work, and the worse it went for her, the better it went for Rusty. The cement mixer they'd been waiting for since seven-thirty that morning had flipped over en route and tied up traffic downtown all morning. Rusty liked anything that caused delays. Dorian was under pressure to bring the job in on time, and anything that threw the schedule off automatically gave Rusty an edge to negotiate for overtime from the city. Anything that made the engineer look incompetent, the contractor danced a jig over. By quitting time Dorian was exhausted and nearly out of patience.

She drove to Lorraine and Abby's house and managed to get herself in a better mood by thinking about Lorraine — Lorraine with a water hose in her pants, Lorraine in the doorway of Abby's room, Lorraine holding her wineglass, Lorraine draped in a toga, Lorraine *un*draped in a toga.

Don't get carried away here, Dorian reminded herself. *She's still in love with Tess.*

Lorraine answered the door. "Great timing. I just put the pasta on. Hey, are you okay?"

Dorian laughed. "I'm okay. It's been a long day."

"How about a drink? Some wine maybe?"

"I'm afraid I'd go right to sleep. Really. I'm fine."

Abby came in with a folder and sat down beside Dorian on the sofa. "Rainey and I went to the library today and got articles on the shipwreck. We're really going, aren't we?"

"Yes," Dorian said. "We're really going." She glanced up from the folder to see Lorraine leaning against the door to the kitchen. Their eyes met. Dorian smiled and then forced herself to look away from her and focus her attention on Abby again.

The folder contained articles about the excavation as well as the history of the ship. It was interesting reading, and Abby's running monologue made it even more enlightening. Abby asked questions about the boat ride and the cofferdam. A while later over spaghetti, the flow of conversation continued with Abby's questions and either Dorian's or Lorraine's answers. By the time they were finished with dinner, Dorian felt as if every inch of the shipwreck and the wonders of marine engineering had been thoroughly covered, and the overall enthusiasm was high.

"This is great spaghetti," Dorian said finally.

"Thanks. I'm glad you like it."

"Sounds like we're ready for Saturday," Dorian said. "I'm glad you two agreed to go with me. It should be fun."

"We're very excited about it, aren't we, kiddo?" Lorraine said. She went to the kitchen and returned with chocolate pudding for dessert. "So you and your brother are both engineers?"

"I actually have four brothers who are engineers."

Lorraine's pudding spoon stopped in midair on its way to her mouth. "Five engineers in your family."

Dorian laughed. "My father's an engineer too, but he's retired."

The questions that followed were personal but not intimate, and Dorian noticed how good Lorraine was at getting her to talk about herself. Before they knew it, Abby was asleep on the sofa and it was ten-thirty.

"I need to get going," Dorian said. "Dinner was great."

They set a departure time for Saturday morning, and Dorian reminded her to bring jackets for the boat ride. On the way home Dorian found herself thinking of the pictures of Tess all over Lorraine's house and how much of her still seemed to be there.

"Friends," Dorian said out loud as she parked her car at her apartment complex. "We're becoming friends and nothing more."

Chapter Six

Saturday morning Dorian was there at eight sharp and was pleased to find them ready. Abby came out of her room in a light blue sweat suit and her hard hat. Seeing her wear it never failed to make Dorian laugh.

"Anybody need to go to the bathroom?" Lorraine asked. It was one of the few times Dorian thought she actually sounded like a mother.

Dorian put their things in the back of her Jeep Cherokee and off they went. She handed Abby a sketch of the cofferdam with easy instructions on how it worked. Lorraine, however, was busy flipping through the CDs Dorian had.

"You like classical music," Lorraine said. "Everything about you surprises me."

"Really? Why?"

"You're never what I'm expecting." She selected a CD and turned the volume down low. "When I'm not around you, I've got it in my mind that you're sort of butch. The hard hat, the boots, the things Abby tells me about you."

"What things?" Dorian asked. She had Dorian's attention now, but Lorraine turned and looked in the back seat.

"She's asleep already," Lorraine said. "Moving vehicles do that to her after about three miles. She's a lot of fun cross-country."

"What has Abby told you?" Dorian asked again. She had been called a lot of things in her life, but "butch" wasn't one of them.

"You're the boss," Lorraine said. "The way you're always telling those men what to do. Abby thinks that's great." Lorraine must have seen something in Dorian's expression, because she started talking a little faster. "It's just this mental image I had of you . . . without knowing you or even meeting you. And the more I'm around you, the fuzzier that mental picture gets." Lorraine glanced out the passenger window. "I'm sure you've worked very hard to get where you're at, and the men you work with either respect you or despise you. None of that is easy. Am I right?"

"Yes," Dorian said. "Basically."

Phil Cohen and Dorian's coworkers at Cohen Engineering did respect her and always had. She wasn't sure how much Phil himself had to do with it, but Dorian pulled her weight and she knew what she was doing. She had earned the right to be where she was.

"Are you out to your family?" Lorraine asked.

"Not all of them yet," Dorian said. "I'm out to my parents, and I've told this particular brother and his wife, but I haven't gotten around to the others. Everybody's so busy, and it's not the sort of thing I want to do on the phone. How about you?" she asked. "How are things with your family?"

"Before Tess died I think they were embarrassed about me being a lesbian, but they're into the PFLAG thing now and are doting grandparents. Tess's family disowned her after she came out." Lorraine gazed out the window. "I called to let them know when the funeral was, but they didn't come. It took them several weeks before they even asked how she died," Lorraine said. "That's when they found out about Abby. I didn't hear from them again for a while. Several years, in fact." She looked out the window once more. "My parents were great when Tess died. That's what really brought us together as a family."

"So you've had Abby from day one," Dorian said.

Lorraine smiled. "I brought her home from the hospital. I don't know if Tess sensed something would happen or if fate was at work, but the papers for me to adopt Abby were signed before Tess got so sick. It's strange how things work out."

"You adopted her right away," Dorian said.

"At Tess's insistence. Like she knew something would happen. She died of an embolism five hours later." Lorraine's voice took on a huskiness that made

Dorian uncomfortable. She decided to change the subject, but Lorraine cleared her throat and continued talking before Dorian had a chance to talk about anything else.

"One of the biggest arguments my mother and I ever had came about a year later," Lorraine continued with a smile. "Abby was learning to talk, and I was having trouble deciding what I wanted her to call me. Tess was her mother, and I wanted Abby to always know that. It didn't seem right having Abby call me mom, so I taught her to say Rainey. For all intents and purposes, I'm her mother and she's my daughter, but it was important to me that she know Tess, the woman who gave birth to her and loved her enough and wanted her enough to —"

She stopped for a moment and then said, "It was just very important to me that Tess's role in Abby's life not be forgotten. And my mother thought that was too weird to deal with. She slips a 'go ask your mother' in as often as she can. Abby has always referred to Tess as her mom, and she doesn't think it strange when other people refer to me as her mother. And Abby's the only person other than Tess who's ever called me Rainey." She laughed nervously and glanced over at Dorian. "I've told you more in the last five minutes than I've ever told anyone. Let's talk about you now." Lorraine ran her fingers through the front of her blonde hair and propped her elbow up on the back of the seat. "How long have you been single?"

Dorian wasn't sure she wanted to get into any of that, but Lorraine had been brutally honest with her. "My last relationship ended badly," Dorian said. "Gina was married and lied about it. I didn't find out until she told me she was pregnant with her husband's baby. I stopped seeing her. That was over a year ago."

"Have you started dating again?" Lorraine asked. "I can see where trust issues would be a problem after something like that."

Dorian shrugged. "I go out with friends and co-workers, but I haven't really dated anyone. It's pretty scary out there these days."

Lorraine laughed. "Tell me about it. You sleep with anyone, and she wants to move in before lunch."

During the rest of the trip they talked more about their families and Abby. After they'd covered that territory, Lorraine asked Dorian to explain exactly how the cofferdam worked.

They arrived at the huge beach house at ten-thirty after several unsuccessful attempts to interpret the directions Dorian had written down. Dorian's patience and determination to find the place without calling for additional directions made Lorraine snicker more than once.

"Maybe you're a lot butchier than I thought," Lorraine said. "That's a man-thing. The inability to ask for directions."

"And let me remind you that you're stereotyping me, and that's very unbecoming." Dorian nodded toward the back seat. "How long will she sleep like that?"

"Until the car stops," Lorraine said. "It's amazing. I'll never have to worry about her becoming a truck driver."

"What's wrong with truck drivers?"

"Oh, forget it."

It was Dorian's turn to smirk. "By the way," she said, "just so it doesn't take you by surprise later, my brother's name is Joseph and his wife's name is Mary. They're used to the ribbing. It doesn't bother them, but I thought you'd want to know ahead of time."

"Mary and Joseph," Lorraine said, then added under her breath, "Jesus."

"Actually," Dorian said, "they don't have any children yet."

Dr. Mary Sadler was a petite redhead with an engaging smile and piercing green eyes. She met them at the front door and gave Dorian a big hug. Dorian introduced Lorraine and a now wide-awake Abby, who needed to use the bathroom.

"We'll take my Jeep to the boat," Mary said. "Grab jackets and sunscreen if you've got it. If not we'll find something on the boat."

The top was off the old and rusted Jeep. A steady wind whipped up from the Gulf, and the sun felt good. Dorian remembered the Jeep well from other visits she'd made in various parts of the country. Lorraine and Abby crawled in the back seat.

"We've only got about two more weeks before our funding runs out," Mary said. "And hurricane season is right around the corner." She smiled at Dorian while shifting gears. Mary was Dorian's favorite sister-in-law, which was one reason she had come out to her several years ago. Dorian had confided in Mary about her lesbianism even before she had told her brother.

"He's been looking forward to seeing you," Mary said. "We're glad you could come."

"Why can't you get more funding?" Dorian asked. "There seems to be a lot of interest in this project. The news coverage in south Texas alone should be worth some big bucks."

Mary smiled. "Mainly because we're almost finished. We could probably squeeze another few weeks out of them, but the weather's very unpredictable now and tourist season is approaching. The local merchants love us because we're bringing in business, but the shrimpers aren't happy. A large part of the bay is off limits to them now. Here we go," she said and parked the Jeep next to a dock.

As everyone crawled out, Dorian thumped Abby's hard hat and said, "Hey, you stayed awake that time."

"Under three miles," Lorraine reminded Dorian.

Since Dorian had seen the boat before, she knew what to do to help Mary get them under way. Dorian helped Abby and Lorraine with their life jackets and showed them the best places to sit. The site was a ten-minute ride out, and Mary pointed toward porpoises frolicking in the channel. Abby was so excited she couldn't sit still, but Lorraine kept an arm around her shoulder and delighted in showing her other things along the way. Mary let them know which direction they'd be able to see the cofferdam from, and slowed the boat as they approached.

The site was impressive even from six hundred yards away, and the closer they got, the more ingenious the whole concept appeared. Out in the middle of the bay the shipwreck was completely surrounded by the cofferdam — a structure one hundred and forty-eight feet long and one hundred and eighteen feet wide. The cofferdam was formed by concentric walls of nearly a half-inch-thick steel plates. The bay water had been pumped out, leaving the ship's remains on dry land. It was an engineering masterpiece, only the second one ever constructed. Dorian couldn't stop smiling the closer they came to it. On impulse, she gave Mary a quick hug.

After securing the boat, Dorian helped Lorraine and Abby onto another small dock.

"Wow," Abby said. "Did you see that fish jump over there? Are any sharks out here, Dorian? Like *Jaws*?"

"Sharks maybe," she said, "but not like *Jaws*."

From the walkway along the top of the cofferdam the four of them peered down at the workers below. Everyone wore either a yellow or white hard hat, and all were clustered to the left of the small ship.

Lorraine leaned over next to Dorian, her right breast grazing Dorian's upper arm, and said, "Look at all those construction workers down there."

Dorian rolled her eyes and then chuckled.

"This is so exciting," Lorraine said after a moment. "Tess would've loved it." She put her hands on Abby's shoulders and pulled her close in front of her. "Thanks for sharing it with us."

A young woman in khaki shorts and a T-shirt arrived with hard hats for everyone. She was tall like Dorian and had a friendly smile. Dorian assumed she was an archaeology student.

"I've arranged for a more personal tour for you two," Mary said to Lorraine and Abby as she passed out hard hats. She put hers on as well. Mary's green eyes twinkled as she looked down at Abby. "I see at least one of you came prepared."

Dorian put her hat on and met Lorraine's amused expression. "You, too, can be a construction worker," Dorian noted.

"And tell me again why I need to wear this?" Lorraine asked.

"A safety precaution," Mary replied. "It'll keep the sea gull crap out of your hair." She turned and introduced the archaeology student as Consuelo. "She'll show you two the most recent artifacts we've uncovered and explain what we do around here. Any questions she can't answer, we'll find someone who can."

"Where will you be, Dorian?" Abby asked, squinting up at her into the sun. The wind off the Gulf was cooperating enough to blow her hair out of her face.

"I need to find my brother and talk about engineering stuff for a while," Dorian said. "I'll see you later."

Abby and Lorraine, holding hands and asking questions already, went off with Consuelo. As soon as they were out of earshot, Mary asked Dorian how long she and Lorraine had been an item.

"We're not," Dorian said. "We're just friends."

Mary eyed her with a perfectly arched brow. "Which one of us are you kidding? Me or you?"

"We're friends. Nothing more."

"Nothing more *yet*. I've seen the way she looks at you."

Dorian laughed, dismissing the idea. "Since when did you become an expert on how two women look at each other?"

"It's all the same no matter what gender you are," Mary informed her. "Just remember who saw it first."

They found Joseph in the pump room talking to a

mechanic. He stopped in mid-sentence, gave Dorian a hug and introduced her to the two men working there with him. It had been almost a year since Dorian had seen him. He and Mary had spent Christmas working on the *LaBelle* project, missing the usual Sadler family gathering in Dallas. His hair was a little grayer than she remembered, but he still had plenty of it to complement the rest of his tan, lean frame. He and Mary made a handsome couple.

By the end of the day Dorian and Lorraine both admitted that it didn't seem strange at all that they were standing on the bottom of Matagorda Bay next to the remains of a three hundred-year-old shipwreck. The silt that had washed in and covered the wreck over the years had helped preserve everything. The *LaBelle* had been a major find, and Mary confirmed that there were still surprises waiting for them everyday.

"That's where they found the skeleton, Dorian," Abby said, pointing toward the ribs of the ship. "And cannons, too." She stood between Dorian and Lorraine and reached up to take their hands. Even with sunscreen on, Abby was showing signs of too much sun.

"We're finished here for the day," Joseph said. "I'm buying dinner. How does seafood sound?"

On the boat ride back, Abby chattered the entire way. Lorraine had several questions of her own to ask and kept Mary engaged in conversation.

"Will the cofferdam come down when you're finished here?" Lorraine asked, "or will you just pump water back in and leave it?"

"Leaving it as it is would be too dangerous," Mary said. "We'll dismantle it."

Back on dry land, Dorian helped Joseph secure the

boat and put their life jackets away. Lorraine and Dorian then got into the back of the Jeep with Abby between them.

"I hope everybody's hungry," Joseph said on the way to the restaurant. They chose a table out by the water and left in pairs for the rest room to wash the grit away. Dorian could feel the silt and salt on her face, and was looking forward to a shower when she got home.

Drinks were brought and orders were taken. Joseph and Dorian talked about the family while Mary and Lorraine continued discussing the *LaBelle*. Even after their food arrived the chatter continued, and Dorian asked Abby what she liked best that day.

"The cannons," she said excitedly. "They didn't look like cannons with all those skunky barbells on 'em."

"Barnacles," Lorraine said, correcting her. "Not barbells. Barnacles."

"All those skunky barnacles," Abby said.

Chapter Seven

Even though Joseph and Mary tried to convince them to stay another day, Dorian insisted that they needed to get back. She promised herself, as well as her brother, that she'd see them again soon when they could spend more time together.

"They're very nice people," Lorraine said once they were on the road again, her head resting back on the seat. Abby was already asleep. "You and your brother look a lot alike," she said. "Especially around the eyes."

"We all look like that," Dorian said.

"Where do you fall in the pack?"

Dorian laughed. "I'm the baby."

"Four older brothers? I bet they spoiled you rotten."

"Not so you'd notice."

"How'd your mother handle hearing that her only daughter is a lesbian?"

Dorian shrugged. "She cried at first, but we worked it out in a few hours. It's not what they would've chosen for me, but my parents love me. They want me to be happy."

"Are you?" Lorraine asked.

"I like my job. I'm doing what I was trained to do."

"That's your answer?"

"Is anyone ever really happy?" Dorian countered. "I guess in a way I've had spurts of what you'd call happiness. Right now I'm content with being content."

"I know what you mean," Lorraine said. The dim light from the dashboard did little to illuminate the front seat. Lorraine's features and expression weren't readable. "I've been happier in my life, but I can't say that I'm unhappy right now."

She went on to talk about Tess and what their life together had been like. Lorraine confessed that it had taken a long time for her to realize that Tess was actually gone forever.

"I was in shock those first few months," she admitted. "Abby needed my full attention, and I gave her everything I had left. She became my whole life at a time when I desperately needed something." Lorraine turned her head and smiled at Dorian. "Today was fun. We both felt very special."

"I'm glad. I had fun too."

Lorraine was looking at her in a way that made Dorian warm around the collar and made her foot begin to pat on its own.

"Joseph and Mary are interesting people," Dorian said after a moment. "Their lives are full of adventure."

Dorian had expected both of her passengers to fall asleep on the way back since it had been a long, busy day followed by a huge meal, but Lorraine was awake and curious. She continued talking about Tess and asked more questions about Dorian's ex-lover. Dorian preferred not to discuss Gina and their disastrous twelve months together, and it was easy to turn the conversation back to either Tess or Abby. Before either of them realized it, two hours had passed and they were approaching the city limits of San Antonio.

When Dorian parked in Lorraine's driveway, the clock in the Jeep read ten-thirty. Dorian offered to carry a sleeping Abby in the house while Lorraine dug in her pocket for her house key.

"They're a lot heavier when they're asleep," Lorraine said as she fumbled with the lock in the dark.

Once inside Lorraine turned on a few lights and led the way to Abby's room. Dorian was surprised that Abby didn't wake up when her shoes were pulled off.

"You take care of this," Dorian said quietly as Lorraine slipped Abby's shirt over her head. "I'll get the rest of your things and bring them in."

The light from the living room cast just far enough out into the yard to help Dorian find her way safely. Dorian retrieved Abby's hard hat and Lorraine's backpack and brought them in. She set them on the sofa and pulled her keys from her pocket as Lorraine returned from Abby's room.

"She's out for the night," Lorraine said. She reached for Dorian's keys and dropped them on the coffee table, then took Dorian's face in her hands and kissed her deeply.

Dorian was swirling with emotion inside; their lips and tongues did all the talking for them. Dorian's mouth moved to Lorraine's throat and shoulder, where a hint of sweat, mixed with Gulf salt and sunscreen lingered.

"You can stay, can't you?" Lorraine whispered breathlessly as she unbuttoned Dorian's shirt.

"Yes."

"Right answer." Her hands found Dorian's breasts and reached around to unhook her bra. "I'm not sure I'd let you leave even if you wanted to." She found Dorian's mouth again, and heat rushed between Dorian's legs. Lorraine sucked on her tongue. "This way," she said, breaking the kiss and taking Dorian's hand.

The next thing Dorian knew they were in Lorraine's bedroom, kissing again and taking each other's clothes off. No one had touched Dorian this way in months. Not since Gina. Lying, cheating Gina. But Lorraine wasn't Gina, and that made all the difference.

Dorian got Lorraine's shorts and underwear off and urged her on the bed. She lay on top of her and buried her face in Lorraine's breasts, kissing them and tugging on her nipples with her lips.

"Take your clothes off," Lorraine said. "All of them. I need to feel you on me."

Dorian covered Lorraine's mouth with her own and began another series of deep, hungry kisses. Dorian could feel Lorraine squirming beneath her, begging to be touched.

Dorian kissed Lorraine's breasts, pausing long enough to tease her nipples again before moving down farther.

"Damn you," Lorraine mumbled. She had her hands on the sides of Dorian's head and her fingers woven through dark curls as Dorian's mouth continued to caress her body. The mumbled cursing turned to soft moaning the moment Dorian's tongue sank between Lorraine's opened thighs. She was wet and ready, and came much too quickly as far as Dorian was concerned. Lorraine tugged on Dorian's ear and then ran her fingers through the top of her hair, gripping it firmly several times, but not really pulling on it. She finally let go of her and pushed two pillows under her head. She looked at Dorian, who still lingered between her legs, and said, "You only get away with that once."

"Get away with what?"

"Take your clothes off and get up here," Lorraine said playfully.

Dorian smiled and took her shoes off, but didn't bother with anything else. Her shirt was unbuttoned and her bra unfastened, but both were still technically on. Dorian's jeans, however, weren't even unzipped yet. She kissed the tops of Lorraine's thighs and her stomach before taking her own shirt and bra off the rest of the way. Dorian had every intention of getting completely undressed and then making love to her again, but Lorraine had other ideas.

"Oral sex makes me come too fast," Lorraine said.

She had Dorian on her back and took a breast in her hand and rubbed the nipple with her thumb. "And I want it to be slow with you," she said. "Slow."

She brought her warm, wet mouth down and took the nipple between her lips while moving her hand to the top of Dorian's jeans. Lorraine eased the zipper down and slipped her palm inside Dorian's underwear.

"You're as ready as I was," Lorraine said. "Good. Now let's get rid of these, shall we?"

They got Dorian out of her clothes and rolled on the bed, locked in a kiss with legs entwined and hands rubbing and caressing soft flesh.

"Oh god, you feel good," Lorraine whispered. She got a knee in between Dorian's legs and then slipped two fingers inside of her.

"I can't come this way," Dorian said.

"Show me how then. Please."

They rolled over again with Dorian on top of her. She got one of Lorraine's legs between her own and opened herself up with her fingers. Dorian was very wet, and she began slowly sliding on Lorraine's lower thigh.

"Oh yes, baby," Lorraine cooed in her ear. "You feel so good." She managed to capture one of Dorian's nipples and sucked hard. "That's it, baby," Lorraine said breathlessly as Dorian began to move faster, grinding herself into that wonderful wet thigh. "That's it. God you feel good."

Dorian couldn't remember an orgasm so strong, so wild and consuming. Her body trembled afterward, and Lorraine held her until the trembling stopped.

"That was inspiring," Lorraine said as she kissed Dorian's sweaty forehead and chuckled. "You have a way of getting me so hot."

"Then let's see what we can do about it." Dorian began kissing her again, playfully at first and then more seriously as they kept at it.

"I want your mouth on me again," Lorraine whispered urgently. "But don't let me come." She kissed Dorian deeply, her mouth fully open and her tongue searching. She broke away from the kiss and whispered, "When I start getting close, use your fingers on me. Your fingers in me and your tongue on me."

Lorraine's kisses became wild and passionate, as if just talking about how she wanted to be made love to was all she needed. Dorian had been given a dose of inspiration as well. It was a fun and enlightening evening, and morning came much too quickly.

Dorian heard Lorraine talking to someone and opened an eye to make sure they were still alone. Lorraine hung up the phone and then kissed her on the cheek.

"Go back to sleep. I'll only be a few minutes."

Through her opened eye she watched as Lorraine pulled on a pair of sweats and left the room. Dorian went to the bathroom and then returned to bed and fell asleep again. It seemed like only minutes before Lorraine came back.

"Is Abby up?" Dorian asked sleepily.

Lorraine took her clothes off and crawled back into bed.

"I called Ethan and told him to pick her up for breakfast and then take her to the zoo. He's been promising to do it for months, and today seemed like the perfect time." She ran a hand over Dorian's thigh. "That means we can spend the whole day here. Doing this."

"We should be exhausted," Dorian said. She reached for her and kissed her. They made love again; exhaustion could wait a while longer.

They took showers later that afternoon with every intention of having a nice leisurely breakfast, but they didn't even make it to the coffeepot before they were back in bed again. There was too much to learn about each other, and their time alone together was limited.

Dorian liked the way Lorraine used her hair when she made love to her, lightly sweeping it over her skin with feathery touches. Lorraine was a persistent, curious lover and seemed to enjoy discovering new ways to bring Dorian pleasure.

"You've got a nice body," Lorraine said. She was on top of Dorian, kissing her throat and shoulder as she slowly eased her way down. She let her hair dance over Dorian's breasts and then slipped a knee between Dorian's legs, but she kept her immediate focus on hard nipples brought to life by the flick of a tongue. "You've got great muscle tone, too," she whispered. "If

I hadn't been so pissed the first time I saw you I might've mentioned it then."

She continued to whisper while nibbling at Dorian's stomach and stringing kisses along and below her navel. Lorraine worked her other knee between Dorian's and then wasted no time spreading Dorian's legs and burying her tongue inside of her.

Dorian's response was immediate. She brought her legs up and filled her hands with Lorraine's silky hair. The sensation was powerful and intoxicating, and within seconds Dorian was ready to come.

She gripped the edge of the pillow with one hand and had the other on the back of Lorraine's head as she began moving her hips in rhythm. The stroking stopped abruptly, and Dorian heard Lorraine say, "Whoa, whoa, whoa."

"Jesus, don't stop!" Dorian panted. "Please. Don't —"

"Slow down, babe," Lorraine said. "Why didn't you tell me you liked this so much?"

Dorian grabbed the sheet in frustration. "Do we have to talk about this now?"

Lorraine resumed stroking her with the tip of her tongue slowly, and Dorian was eventually able to regain the momentum and excitement she'd lost. She came with a long gravelly moan, and felt limp and exhausted afterward. Lorraine was beside her quickly, in Dorian's arms kissing her cheek and lips over and over again.

"Why didn't you tell me last night?" Lorraine asked. She brushed sweaty curls away from Dorian's forehead. "I like brutal honesty in bed. I can't be a good lover if you don't tell me what you like."

"Jesus," Dorian said. "You'd be a good lover no matter what I told you."

Lorraine smiled and propped her head up with her hand. "How so?"

"You're very confident about what you want, and you're not embarrassed to vocalize it. I'm not used to it, but I certainly like it."

Lorraine kissed Dorian fully on the mouth. "It doesn't make any sense not to help with directions when you know the way." Lorraine chuckled and playfully bit Dorian's lip. "You learn fast. I like that."

Chapter Eight

The telephone rang at five-thirty that afternoon and woke them up; Ethan was bringing Abby home.

"When will they be here?" Dorian asked. She threw the covers off and was ready to get up and get dressed, but Lorraine rolled on top of her and began kissing her again.

"Twenty minutes or so," Lorraine said. Her tongue outlined Dorian's ear, sending a wave of goose bumps along her flesh.

"Shouldn't we be getting dressed?" Dorian managed to say.

"We will. We will."

Dorian, the taller and stronger of the two, rolled Lorraine over on her back. "I don't think I should be here when Abby comes home."

Lorraine stopped squirming under her. "Why?"

"I just don't."

Lorraine reached up and smoothed Dorian's thick, dark curls away from her face. "I was hoping you'd stay with me again tonight," she said, "but maybe you're right."

They both got out of bed and started looking for their clothes. Dorian slipped on her loafers and remembered that her keys were in the living room. Lorraine looked a little disappointed, but Dorian thought she was adorable in gray sweats and white socks.

At the door Lorraine put her arms around Dorian's neck and kissed her again. "I forgot that my kid has a crush on you. I need to have a little talk with her later."

As their kisses became more serious, Dorian reluctantly stepped back away from her. "I should go. Right now."

"Come by tomorrow after work," Lorraine said. "And bring a change of clothes. I've got plans for you."

Dorian arrived at the office early Monday morning and found Mia making coffee. They had, without a doubt, the best smelling office in town — between the coffeepot, fresh flowers and Mia's perfume, there was no contest.

"You get the first cup," Mia said. She handed Dorian a steaming cup of coffee and then gave her the three telephone messages that she'd taken in the last twenty minutes.

"Did the hard hat fit?" Mia asked. "They promised me it was the smallest they had."

"Yes!" Dorian said. "I forgot to tell you. Yes. It fit perfectly, and it was a big hit. Thanks again for finding it."

Mia smiled. "You're in a good mood this morning." She nodded toward the three messages. "Traffic congestion on Oak Street. That's the big complaint so far."

Dorian took the messages and glanced at them. "Rusty's probably got the backhoe in the middle of the street again with no detour signs up."

Mia shook her head and tossed her hair over a shoulder. "You and Rusty are still going at it?"

"As long as we're both breathing we'll be going at it."

Dorian took care of those three calls and then had two more to handle before she could leave. Another heart-to-heart talk with Rusty was on her agenda as soon as she arrived at the site. She needed to remind him that a little forethought and courtesy in the neighborhood would go a long way.

"Courtesy my butt," he grumbled when she told him. He shifted his nasty, soggy cigar to the other side of his jaw. "I found those damn dipsticks from my bulldozers this mornin'. A bunch of kids down the street were having a sword fight with 'em. What kind of courtesy is *that*?"

"And how do you suppose they got the dipsticks?" she asked him calmly.

"Beats me, Ms. Sadler. Don't you check the security of this place at night?"

"Yes, I do," Dorian said. She stuck her pen on her clipboard and continued. "Maybe you should look into hiring a full-time security guard at night. I might have to make that recommendation in the future."

The cigar shifted to the other side of Rusty's mouth almost on its own accord. "No need for that," he said, immediately seeing where she was going with this. A security guard would come out of Rusty's pocket, and he wasn't about to get caught up in that. But if Dorian were to make the recommendation to the city manager, then it was as good as done.

Rusty did an about-face and crawled in his truck. *At least he knows when to shut up*, Dorian thought.

Abby wasn't waiting for her when they stopped working for the day. Dorian wondered how Lorraine's talk with her had gone.

She changed out of her work boots and put on her new Doc Martens. Keeping her mind on work and off of Lorraine had taken a lot of concentration most of the day, but Rusty and his crew had been more of a diversion than Dorian would've liked.

Dorian parked in front of Lorraine's house behind an unfamiliar car and noticed two others in the driveway. Ethan answered the door and let her in. His hair was wet, his feet were bare, and an older woman was arguing with him.

Dorian noticed right away that three conversations were going on at once in the living room, and she didn't see Lorraine or Abby anywhere. Felicia was on the phone in an intense conversation, adding to the chaos. Abby's bedroom door opened, and she came out in a huff, her hair wet and neatly combed. Lorraine came out right behind her with a furrowed brow and arms crossed over her chest. Dorian immediately surmised that this was *not* a place that she needed to be.

Felicia put her hand over the phone and asked Lorraine if she could make a ten-thirty appointment in the morning.

"Yes," Lorraine said. "Ten-thirty's fine." Her expression changed when she saw Dorian. She smiled tiredly and took Dorian by the hand and led her to the bedroom. The moment the door closed, Lorraine was in her arms kissing her.

"Please tell me you've come to take me away from all of this," she whispered in Dorian's ear. She found Dorian's mouth again and put her arms around her neck. "This is the best thing that's happened to me all day."

"Same here," Dorian said.

Each long, deep kiss was only a prelude to the turmoil in Dorian's body. She knew they couldn't make love now, but with Lorraine's tongue darting in and out of her mouth that way, anything seemed possible.

Lorraine's lips moved down to Dorian's throat. "Do you have to go back to the office?" she whispered.

"Yes," Dorian said huskily. "I stopped by on my way. I had to see you."

Lorraine undid Dorian's top three buttons on her shirt and cupped her breast. She then leaned her head on Dorian's chest and laughed softly.

"What the hell am I doing?" Lorraine whispered.

"I can't keep my hands off of you. Christ. What a lousy day I've had." She buttoned up Dorian's shirt and kissed her quickly on the mouth one last time. "Why don't you take care of the office now while I get rid of these people and tend to a few things? Some weird stuff happened today, and I'd like to talk it over with you later. You can come back, can't you?" Lorraine touched the front of Dorian's hair in a shy caress. "And stay the night?" she whispered. "I have to see you. Please."

"I'll be back," Dorian said. They looked at each other with smoldering passion, but they knew better than to touch again. Dorian opened the door and went back to the craziness that had engulfed the living room. Except for Felicia's glare, Dorian thought it possible that she herself had become invisible.

The office had been quiet even though the other two engineers were in sorting through mail and returning their own stack of phone messages. Dorian finished what she could and left a few things for Mia. She decided to go home and take a shower before returning to Lorraine's house. She wanted to make sure that the circus she'd stumbled upon earlier was indeed gone already.

When she finally arrived at Lorraine and Abby's, she found them on the front porch looking through the telescope.

"We're waitin' for the moon," Abby said. "It's behind that cloud."

Lorraine tousled Abby's hair. "And it's been there for quite a while."

"I got in trouble today," Abby confessed with a sigh. "I accidentally squirted Grandma with my water gun."

"Accidentally?" Lorraine said. "You *emptied* it on her." She took another peek in the telescope. "I think we've seen the last of the moon for the night, kiddo. It's bedtime."

Dorian offered to bring the telescope in. Abby reached over and put her arms around her neck for a hug. "You smell good," she said.

Lorraine laughed heartily. "Come on. Off to bed."

Dorian stood the telescope at the end of the sofa while Lorraine tucked Abby in. The pictures on the mantel caught Dorian's attention again, and she studied them more closely this time. One picture of Lorraine and Tess had been taken at Christmas and used as a Christmas card. Lorraine was obviously younger in the picture, but she hadn't changed that much. Tess was an attractive woman with dark, shoulder-length hair, brown eyes and a nice smile. Dorian's attention, however, was drawn back to how much Abby looked like Lorraine. Abby's eyes were blue like Lorraine's, and her hair was the same color and texture. Chin, nose, mouth . . . there were many things about Lorraine that were prominent in Abby.

She studied another picture that had been taken on the front porch. Tess and Lorraine were sitting on the top step squinting into the sun, their arms locked and faces beaming. The frame was silver and had the words *To Have and to Hold* engraved across the bottom.

"What do you see?" Lorraine asked, slipping her hand into Dorian's.

"Two happy people."

"We were. Very happy." She put her arms around Dorian's neck and said, "Mmm. Abby's right. You do smell good."

Dorian kissed her throat and reminded her that there was something she'd wanted to talk about earlier.

"Yes," Lorraine whispered. "But later." She kissed Dorian deeply, and Dorian's knees turned to jelly. "Bed," Lorraine mumbled. "We're going to bed first."

"Are you sure? You were very upset earlier."

"Positive."

Dorian followed Lorraine to her room, where they shed their clothes and tumbled into bed. They made love with the same urgency as before, but with more confidence in what they were doing. It had been a long time since Dorian had been with someone so focused on pleasing her. Gina had been tuned to her own needs, and Dorian had fallen in love with her. Things were now becoming more obvious as Lorraine brought her closer and closer to the edge of orgasm. Gina had been a selfish lover, and Dorian had let her get away with it — and in a way had probably even encouraged it — but Dorian sensed that such an arrangement would not be possible with Lorraine. If they didn't come together, then they would at least come separately.

Afterward Lorraine rested her head on Dorian's shoulder, snug in her arms with the side of her foot slowly moving up and down Dorian's calf.

"I had a lousy day," Lorraine said. "How about you?"

"Just the usual. Probably better than some. They didn't break any water mains." She kissed the top of

Lorraine's head and gave her a hug. "What happened today?"

Lorraine pulled the cover up over them better. "Tess's mother called me this morning. She wants custody of Abby."

Dorian hugged her a little closer and felt an uneasiness in her stomach. She'd had no idea how serious things had been earlier.

"Felicia found a lawyer for me and made the mistake of telling my parents everything when they came over for a surprise visit. Everyone sort of freaked out a little. That's where we were the first time you arrived. Between that and Abby squirting my mother with the water gun, it was a bad day."

"Does Tess's family have a chance to win?"

"They aren't getting my kid," Lorraine said. "I'd pack up and leave before it ever got to that. If anything, these people might finally be missing Tess — the same Tess they threw out of their house for being a lesbian, the same Tess they didn't talk to or care about for five years. She died before any of that was resolved. I won't let people like that get my daughter. It won't happen. They can see her, but they can't have her."

"What does your lawyer say?" Dorian asked.

"My appointment's in the morning. I wouldn't count on this redneck, homophobic state we live in to be on my side, but Felicia swears by this lawyer." Lorraine kissed Dorian's cheek. "Besides. It might not come to any of that. In the heat of anger this morning, I told the old lady I'd sign over custody to Abby's father before I'd let them get their hands on her. I'm sure it gave them something to think about."

"Is Abby's father —"

"It's just a threat, Dorian. No one's taking Abby away from me, and I'm not handing her over to anyone." Lorraine ran her palm slowly over Dorian's stomach. "Tess's mother is probably just lonely right now. Abby's birthday always gets to her pretty bad since it's the same day Tess died."

"You don't think there's much to the custody thing?" Dorian said.

"She meant it at the time," Lorraine said. "And Tess's sister might even have something to do with it, but I'm not really worried. I guess it surprised me more than anything." She kissed Dorian's cheek and then rolled on top of her. "You're very easy to talk to," Lorraine said. She locked her fingers through Dorian's and stretched her arms out and over Dorian's head. Their breasts were touching, teasing each other, and felt absolutely wonderful.

"I think *easy* is the operative word here," Dorian whispered.

Lorraine laughed. "You might be right." She began rocking against her and grinding herself into Dorian's center. "I've been with other women since Tess died." She let go of Dorian's hands and propped herself up better so the rocking could become more serious. "For what it's worth," she whispered, "you're the first one who's ever stayed the night."

Dorian didn't know what to say, but before she had the chance to say anything, they were both reeling from sensation. Dorian grabbed her and pulled her closer, matching the rocking motion with only one goal in mind. They came together, moving wildly and moaning their pleasure out into the night.

* * * * *

Saturday afternoon Dorian, Lorraine and Abby were invited to Felicia's house for a cookout. Dorian wasn't thrilled about going because she sensed that Felicia didn't particularly like her, but she was willing to make the best of it. Lorraine was in charge of the grill, and Dorian had decided earlier that she wanted to spend more time with Abby. The job site Dorian was working on had moved farther away from Lorraine and Abby's neighborhood — too far for Abby to be showing up on her bicycle. Dorian had missed their afternoon talks.

"How's Buster?" Dorian asked. She opened three soda cans and gave one each to Abby and Hank and kept one for herself. She then sat across the picnic table from them.

"He needs a bath," Abby said. "He stinks again."

"Did you have a dog when you were little?" Hank asked. He'd lost a front tooth since Dorian had last seen him.

She nodded and sipped her Diet Coke. Dorian had finally figured out who Hank belonged to. His mother was also a single parent and a good friend of Lorraine's. He spent time at Abby and Lorraine's house when she had to be out of town.

"What was your dog's name?" Abby asked her.

"Ozone," Dorian said. The kids cackled, and Dorian noticed how Lorraine turned away from the grill to look at her. "I had three dogs," Dorian said. "All named Ozone."

"Three dogs at the same *time* named Ozone?" Abby asked.

Dorian nodded again. "Three dogs all named Ozone. Whenever I wanted them to do something I'd yell their name and all three would come running."

The kids giggled again, and then Abby asked, "What if you just wanted one dog at a time? How would they know which one you were callin'?"

"I never wanted just one," Dorian said with a shrug, "so that wasn't a problem."

"But what *if*," Hank insisted. "What *if* you wanted just one."

"Yeah," Lorraine called out, shutting the top of the smoky grill. "What *if?*"

Dorian laughed and sipped her soda. "Like I said. It wasn't a problem."

A while later Lorraine came over to the picnic table and sat down next to Dorian. More women had arrived, most of whom Dorian recognized from the toga party.

"Felicia's new girlfriend's supposed to be here," Lorraine said. "I haven't met her yet." She glanced around the yard. "Where did Abby and Hank go?"

"Sega Genesis," Dorian said. "Felicia has two new games and a big-screen TV. They're having a great time."

Lorraine waved at someone across the yard and motioned Felicia and what appeared to be her new girlfriend over. Dorian and Gina saw each other at the same time. Gina let go of Felicia's hand and stopped in the middle of the yard. Gina. Lying, cheating Gina. Felicia turned and laughed, reaching for Gina's hand again and encouraging her along. Dorian got up from the picnic table and went inside the house. She stood in the kitchen feeling queasy and breathless.

She made a fool out of me, Dorian kept thinking over and over again. *Pretending to love me while she slept with that husband I didn't know she had.*

Dorian had noticed the fear in Gina's eyes moments before she'd pulled her hand away from Felicia's. It was the first time they'd seen each other since their last terrible fight.

The back door opened, and Dorian was afraid that she'd find Gina there, but Lorraine came in instead.

"Are you okay?" Lorraine asked.

Dorian nodded.

"What happened to you out there?" Her puzzled expression made Dorian look away. "That's probably the rudest thing I've ever —"

"I'm sorry," Dorian said. "Look, I'm not feeling very well all of a sudden."

"What's the matter?" Lorraine had her hands on her hips, and her blue eyes were drilling into Dorian. "It's that woman. You know her, don't you? Talk to me, Dorian."

Dorian didn't say anything and wouldn't look at her. She felt nauseous and was willing herself not to throw up.

"Please talk to me," Lorraine said quietly.

They both waited for the silence to end, but neither made an attempt to do anything about it. Finally Lorraine said, "Oh Jesus. Is that *your* Gina out there? The woman you were in love with?" She came closer, moving around in front of Dorian to look at her. "Talk to me," Lorraine said. "That's her, isn't it?"

Dorian closed her eyes and took a deep breath. She had to get out of there.

"Are you still in love with her?" Lorraine asked.

"Love?" Dorian said with a husky whisper. "What the hell is that?"

Lorraine crossed her arms over her chest and followed Dorian's eyes, bobbing her head about until Dorian finally looked at her. "If you weren't still in love with her, you wouldn't be this upset."

"Love," Dorian said. "Gina and I never had love. There was nothing but lies. Yes, I'm upset, but maybe it's because Felicia's getting mixed up with her. Or maybe I'm upset because she reminds me of the worst time in my life. It could be a lot of things, but it sure as hell isn't love."

"You might truly believe that, but I'd say you're wrong, Dorian. You're still in love with her."

"You mean the way you're still in love with Tess?" Dorian asked simply. She regretted saying it the moment it was out of her mouth, but she couldn't take it back. "I'm sorry," Dorian whispered, horrified at her own words. "God, I'm sorry."

Lorraine's eyes were wide with shock.

"Please," Dorian whispered. "Please, forgive me."

"It's okay," Lorraine said. "Are you leaving? Go if you have to. Abby and I have a way home." She turned and walked out of the room.

Chapter Nine

Dorian woke up Monday morning to booming thunder. The electricity was off, so she checked her watch and saw that it was time to get up anyway. At least she wouldn't have to deal with Rusty today.

She had spent most of Sunday with Luke watching movies. He knew she was upset, but he didn't ask any probing questions. *That's what makes him such a good friend,* she thought. *He usually knows when to shut up.*

Dorian kept a battery-powered radio on while she was in the shower. The weatherman promised that thunderstorms would be in the area for the next twenty-four hours, which meant she'd be at the office all day except for a security check that evening on her way home.

She dressed in a long, black skirt and a white cotton blouse. She had enough work at the office to keep her busy through a week's worth of rain, and being there for a day would be a nice change. The electricity came back on before she had to leave. Dorian glanced at her answering machine and saw that there were still no messages. Lorraine hadn't called. *And why should she be the one to call first?* Dorian thought suddenly. *I'm the one who screwed this one up. I left her stranded at a party, for crissakes.*

On the way to work she kept her mind off Lorraine and Abby by concentrating on how she would design drainage projects for certain parts of the city if they had the funds to let her do what she wanted. It was a little game she liked to play during bad weather. The traffic was terrible, but she'd left her apartment early. Mia was already at the office when Dorian got there.

"Hey," Mia said. "No Rusty for you today." She handed over a small stack of papers and a few phone messages. "We missed you at Ruffino's on Saturday."

"Oh," Dorian said. She'd completely forgotten about it.

"Coffee's ready," Mia announced. "I'll bring you some."

There were fresh, pink carnations on her window sill, a welcome sight on such a gloomy day. Dorian set her briefcase on the corner of her desk and scanned her mail. It was nice being in the office, but she knew that by the time the rain ended she'd be ready to get back to the site again.

Mia came in with two cups of coffee and set Dorian's on the desk. She leaned against the door to sip hers and listen for the phone.

"What dirt did I miss on Saturday?" Dorian asked.

Mia laughed. "You know the deal. Whatever we say stays at Ruffino's, but you and Rusty are always a lively topic." She looked at Dorian and smiled. "I was disappointed that you weren't there."

"My weekend would've turned out a lot better had I been."

The telephone at Mia's desk rang, sending her on her way. "You want your door open or closed?"

"Closed," Dorian said. "I hate having you hear me grovel to the fine citizens of San Antonio."

"I'm used to groveling engineers. Doesn't bother me," Mia said as she closed the door.

A steady stream of phone calls came in during the morning, one of them was Rusty complaining about the forecast for the following day as well. A while later, Mia let her know that Phil was in the office since he couldn't play golf in the rain. Twenty minutes later there was a knock on Dorian's door, and Mia came in again.

"There's a woman here to see you." Mia seemed angry, which got Dorian's immediate attention. Mia could handle anything, and over the years she had developed thick skin and the ability to keep her cool no matter how tense or unpleasant the situation could be, so seeing her this way put Dorian on full alert.

"Who is it?" she asked. *An irate neighborhood spokesperson,* Dorian thought. *Someone with chunks out of her sidewalk because of Rusty's nearsighted backhoe operator.*

"That woman," Mia said with nothing less than pure contempt in her voice. Her jaw was set, and fire was in her eyes. "Gina York."

"Gina."

Dorian was stunned for a moment, then her office door swung open and Gina came in with a dripping umbrella. She was dressed to conquer. Her expensive pale gray suit was remarkably dry, but her matching heels weren't quite so lucky.

"I knew you wouldn't see me if I called first," Gina said smoothly. Mia turned and walked out of the office, leaving the door open. Gina leaned her umbrella against the chair in front of Dorian's desk and closed the door with a thud.

"I won't stay long," she said. "I'm here to apologize."

"This isn't the time or the place," Dorian said. She was still in shock at seeing her here.

"It's the *only* time and this is the *only* place," Gina answered. She sat down without being invited to. Dorian could tell that she was nervous by the way she kept patting the back of her nearly perfect hair.

"You wouldn't see me after we broke up, and you refused to return my calls. Then you left the party on Saturday before I could talk to you. We're running in the same circles now. Don't you think we should put all this behind us?"

"If that's what you came to say, then fine. Now leave."

"Dorian, please."

"Please *what*?" Dorian snapped. "You *lied* to me!"

"I *had* to! Would you have seen me then if you'd known about Roger?"

"You already know the answer to that." Dorian leaned back in her chair and stared at the ceiling for a moment, then said, "My most vivid memory of you will always be how I threw my guts up when I discovered you were married. And not just *married*, Gina, but married and pregnant. You were sleeping with both of us at the same time. *That's* how I remember you. Apologize until you turn blue, because it doesn't matter anymore."

Gina sniffed but wouldn't look at her. "You loved me once, Dorian. Can't we salvage anything? Can't we try to be friends?"

"I doubt it. We couldn't build a relationship on lies. Why should a friendship be any different?"

"I've changed, Dorian. Felicia knows everything." Gina paused and then added, "Well, *almost* everything. We're having lunch today, and I'm telling her about you. She doesn't know who my first lesbian lover was." Gina sighed heavily. "As I said before, we seem to know a lot of the same people now. You can't leave every event you see me at."

"Have you said everything you came to say?"

A tear scampered down her cheek, and Gina brushed it away quickly. "Yes. I guess I have." She stood up and reached for her umbrella. "I'm sorry about everything, Dorian. I hope we can be friends some day."

"Right now I don't see how that's possible," Dorian said. She came around her desk to see Gina out before closing the door behind her. "I should've stayed in bed this morning," she mumbled.

* * * * *

Dorian drove to the job site after work and did a quick visual security check. It was still raining, and water was standing everywhere. She made it a point not to drive by Lorraine's house. Maybe there would be a message waiting for her when she got home. *And why should Lorraine be calling me?* Dorian reminded herself again. *I'm the one who should be leaving the messages. I'm the one who screwed this up.*

But the whole thing was still much too raw and awkward. Dorian was embarrassed by the things she'd said, and she wasn't sure what to do about it.

When she got home Luke met her in the hallway outside his apartment and convinced her to have dinner with him. Dorian appreciated the distraction and let him pick the restaurant. Luke had his own melodrama of a life to fill her in on. He was certain that Cedric was seeing someone else on the side, and he wanted her opinion.

"Why don't you just ask him?" Dorian queried.

"What good will *that* do? Besides, I already did and he denied it."

"Oh."

As Luke continued on with his string of suspicions, their food arrived. Dorian's thoughts bounced between Lorraine and Abby and what they were doing right then, but the big mystery of the day — Mia's reaction to Gina's visit that morning — had its own prominent place in Dorian's thoughts. After Gina had left the office that morning, Dorian tried to find Mia and apologize, but she wasn't at her desk. One of the surveyors had been tasked with answering the phone, and when Dorian asked him where Mia had gone he didn't know.

Dorian didn't see her again until after three, and every time she came out of her office to broach the subject, Mia picked up the phone to make a call. Dorian even left her office door open in hopes of catching her in the hallway, but she didn't see her again the rest of the day. Mia left early without bothering to say good-bye, which had never happened during the three years Dorian had worked there. *Now two apologies are in order,* she thought as she poked her baked fish with a fork. *How did I get in this position anyway?*

"Let's go see a movie," Luke said. "Home is too depressing right now." His face brightened, and then he said, "Or we could go dancing. What'll it be? We haven't been dancing in months."

They finally settled on a movie, and by the time Dorian got home it was too late to call Lorraine.

Dorian made it a point to be in the office early the following morning. The thunderstorms had stopped, but were expected to continue again throughout the day.

She went into her office and set her briefcase down, then crossed the hall to the reception area where Mia was.

"Good morning," Dorian said. "Can I talk to you for a minute?"

"Sure. I'll be right there."

After picking up her mail and messages, Dorian

went back to her office. Mia came in behind her and closed the door.

"I'm sorry about what happened yesterday morning," Dorian said. "I know this is an office, and personal —"

"Are you getting back with that woman?" Mia asked. She tossed her hair over her left shoulder and braced her hands on the chair in front of Dorian's desk.

Dorian was surprised by the question and didn't know what to say. Finally Dorian said, "Uh . . . no. That's not my intention at all."

Not only does she know I'm a lesbian, Dorian thought, *she's telling me she knows I'm a lesbian.* This wasn't something that either of them had ever discussed before. Dorian wasn't out at work, but she didn't curtail her activities to keep it a secret either. It was just something that had never come up before.

Mia, however, was visibly relieved by Dorian's answer.

"I've never seen you so upset before," Dorian said. "Is that what you thought was happening?"

"What I think doesn't matter."

"It matters to me," Dorian said. Mia looked up at her for a moment and then looked away again. "Did she make a scene? Were other people around when she was here?"

Mia shook her head. "She was persistent, but no one else was around."

"Okay. Good. I just wanted you to know that I'm sorry you were here when it happened. She won't be back."

Mia left Dorian's office on that note, and things were seemingly back to normal. Dorian knew at some point that she needed to come out at work, but she didn't have time to deal with it now. There was a good chance that there would be a few repercussions when she did, but she hoped that her work would speak for itself when the time came.

"I was on the phone for an hour with Felicia-My-Ex today," Luke said, holding his margarita to his forehead. It always made Dorian laugh to hear him say *Felicia-My-Ex*. It reminded her of movie characters. Like Zorba the Greek, and Jabba the Hut . . . Felicia-My-Ex. Luke collapsed on Dorian's sofa and propped his feet up on the coffee table. "She wanted to know about Gina and you, about you and Gina, about Gina and Roger, about *you* and Roger, and on and on."

"What did you tell her?"

"Not much. She wanted to talk and needed someone to listen. She *did* tell me that you and Lorraine were on the outs." He peeked over at her with a raised eyebrow. "I had to pretend that I knew what she was talking about since I didn't know you and Lorraine were ever *in*, so to speak. So why am I in the dark about her?"

Dorian didn't want to talk about it, but since he told her everything that went on in his life, he apparently thought she should return the favor.

Luke's beeper went off. He checked the number and broke out into a grin. "Prince Charming's on his way home. Gotta go." He drained his glass and kissed her on the cheek. "We'll finish this conversation later. And I want details."

* * * * *

Dorian looked at the phone off and on several times during the rest of the evening and finally got the courage to call Lorraine at eight. She had her apology set and rehearsed, but the moment Lorraine answered the phone amnesia set in.

"Hi," Dorian said, surprised at how nervous she sounded just uttering one word.

"Dorian?" Lorraine said.

"Yes. Hi. Am I calling at a bad time?"

"Not at all."

"How are you?" Dorian asked.

"Better now. It's so good to hear your voice."

Dorian sat down on the sofa and finally began to relax a little. "I'm sorry I —"

"Please don't apologize," Lorraine said. "In a way you were right about a lot of things. I'll always love Tess, but I can't honestly say I'm . . ." She paused and then cleared her throat. "Can you come over? Can we talk about this in person? I'm afraid I'm the one who should be apologizing to you. After spending Saturday afternoon with Gina, I can't imagine you ever being in love with a woman like that. She's manipulative and self-centered. How long were those blinders of yours on?"

Dorian laughed for the first time in days.

"So will you come over?" Lorraine said quietly. "Abby's been asking about you." Then she added, "And I'd like to see you too."

Twenty minutes later Dorian was parked in Lorraine's driveway and running her fingers through her scrambled hair. Abby answered the door in her pajamas and hard hat, which made Dorian laugh.

"We got the pictures back from the shipwreck!" Abby said. She led Dorian to the sofa and squeezed in beside her with the pictures in her lap. Abby started chattering about each one as she pulled it out of the package. Lorraine came into the room and sat on the arm of the sofa next to Dorian. Her fingers touched the back of Dorian's hair in an intimate caress as she leaned over to get a better look.

"Consuelo said we could take pictures," Abby said as she flipped through them. "Rainey had the camera in her jacket in case they didn't want us to, but it was okay."

Lorraine leaned in closer, her body warm and soft against Dorian's shoulder. Dorian saw several pictures that had been taken of her as she talked with her brother on the other side of the cofferdam. Seeing the pictures and knowing that Lorraine had been searching for her then . . . and now feeling Lorraine's fingers slowly toying with her hair . . .

"That's all of 'em," Abby announced as she stacked the pictures in a neat pile. "You wanna see them again?"

Lorraine laughed. "Once is enough, I think." She got up from the arm of the sofa and knelt to help Abby put the pictures back in the package. "She's showed these to Ethan three times already."

"And Grandma and Grandpa once, Felicia once and Hank five times," Abby said. "He likes seeing them too."

"Which one's your favorite?" Dorian asked. She

attempted to concentrate on Abby's enthusiasm as she flipped through the stack again, but from out of nowhere Lorraine's hand was making its way up and down Dorian's leg, obliterating all thought for the moment.

"The one with the barnacles on the cannon!"

"Tell Dorian good-night," Lorraine said. "It's time for bed."

With Lorraine and Abby out of the room, Dorian found herself in front of the mantel again looking at the pictures of Tess and Lorraine. She couldn't imagine losing a lover that way. Hearing Lorraine tell her story about Tess and Abby had made her stop and think more than once. Life was precious, and living it to the fullest while she had a chance had become a new priority of hers.

"I got a call yesterday from Tess's younger sister," Lorraine said a few minutes later. "Abby and I are meeting her for dinner tomorrow night."

"Is she a friend or foe?" Dorian asked.

"She's posing as a friend so far," Lorraine said with a smile. "We'll see." She reached for Dorian's hand and led her to the sofa. "Natalie was just thirteen when Tess died. She's out of college now and curious about Abby."

As Dorian studied Lorraine, it all became very clear to her. There was only one way that Abby and Lorraine could look so much alike without Lorraine being Abby's mother. It suddenly occurred to her that Ethan had to be Abby's father.

Dorian simply asked her, and Lorraine squeezed her hand and then let go of it again.

"Only three people know for sure, believe it or not," Lorraine said. "You, me and Ethan. Others may have figured it out, but haven't said anything. Tess insisted that he be the donor and that we never tell anyone. Including my parents. She wanted Abby to be as much mine as possible." Lorraine smiled tiredly and leaned her head against the back of the sofa. "He's very happy being just Uncle Ethan. And my parents have loved Abby from the beginning. Without even knowing that she's really their biological grand-daughter. It's a win-win situation all around." Lorraine reached over and brushed dark curls away from Dorian's brow. "I've missed you."

"I've missed you too."

"Can you stay tonight?"

"Yes," Dorian said. "I'd like that."

"You've made me do a lot of thinking these last few days," Lorraine admitted. "You were right about Tess and how she's still such a big part of my life. I hadn't realized that before."

"Lorraine, I —"

Lorraine placed a finger on Dorian's lips. "We've talked enough, don't you think?" she whispered. "Come to bed with me." She leaned over and kissed Dorian on the lips, and then gently urged her back on the sofa. An hour later they finally made it to the bed.

Chapter Ten

The following evening Dorian and Luke ordered a pizza and watched a movie at her place. Dorian fell asleep on the sofa and missed the ending, but Luke filled her in as he helped clean up their mess.

"Felicia-My-Ex and Gina-Your-Ex seem to be a hot item these days," he said. "Whatever happened to Roger-the-Husband?"

"Don't know," Dorian said with a yawn. "Ask Felicia about it. She might know."

Luke neatly folded the huge pizza box into the

trash can and rinsed their glasses. "Felicia-My-Ex isn't really talking about this one. And that worries me." He glanced at his watch and swept pizza crumbs off the coffee table into his palm. "Gotta go," he said as he brushed his hands over the trash. "Cedric's due home any minute."

Dorian called Lorraine later to see how dinner with Tess's sister had gone, but there was no answer. She left a message and went to bed.

Lorraine returned her call late the following evening.

"I need to talk to you," she said in an all too serious tone of voice. "Can I come over? Or maybe we could meet somewhere for coffee or something."

"Here's fine," Dorian said. "It doesn't matter. What's wrong? You sound upset."

"I'll tell you when I see you," Lorraine said. "I'll be there in about twenty minutes."

As promised, twenty minutes later Lorraine knocked on her door.

"Where's Abby?" Dorian asked as she let her in.

"At my parents' house. Thanks for seeing me."

Tiny warning bells started going off in Dorian's head. Lorraine looked harried and stressed, and there was a weariness in her eyes that Dorian hadn't seen before. "Sit down. Can I get you something?"

"No, thanks." As Lorraine sat down on the sofa she seemed to be struggling to compose herself.

"What's happened?" Dorian asked. She eased down into the overstuffed chair across from her. "You're scaring me. Is Abby okay? Are you okay?"

"Abby's fine," Lorraine said. "In fact, she'd better be asleep right now." She ran a trembling hand through her hair and then closed her eyes and took a slow, deep breath. "Natalie," she said. "Tess's younger sister. We made love last night."

Dorian felt as though someone had punched her in the stomach. There was no air left in her lungs. She was momentarily dizzy, and everything went in and out of focus.

Lorraine looked at her and then shook her head in disbelief. "There's no one I can talk to about this, Dorian. Felicia's ticked at me because I think Gina's using her. I consider you a good friend. Not just someone I've been sleeping with. And I need to talk right now."

Dorian blinked several times as the shock zoomed through her psyche. Finally she was able to find her voice and managed to say, "Then talk. Please."

Lorraine nodded and rubbed her arms, which were crossed over her chest. "There are two different issues here," she said. "First of all, there's you and me. We've been intimate, and I care about you."

Dorian was determined not to cry. Her entire focus at the moment was zeroed in on that. Lorraine shrugged helplessly.

"I don't play games, Dorian. Being with you has been wonderful. We've been lovers, but we're not —" Lorraine stopped and then looked over at her again. "I just don't want our friendship screwed up over any of this."

Dorian felt numb all over, numb and empty inside. She could feel herself shutting down again. It had first started the day she discovered that Gina had a husband, and it had stayed with her off and on ever since. Lorraine and Abby had been chipping away at this barrier, but it was now firmly back in place.

"Tell me what happened with Natalie," Dorian heard herself saying. She had to know the series of events. Two nights ago Dorian had been in Lorraine's bed, and it had been very good between them. They both knew it and had said so. How could all of that change so quickly? Practically over night? "You and Abby were supposed to have dinner with her," Dorian said.

"I was stunned the entire evening," Lorraine whispered. "Absolutely stunned. From the moment I saw her until she left my house this morning." Lorraine's hands began to tremble again as she nervously raked her fingers through her hair. "I'd only seen her maybe twice at the most. The last time was the summer before Tess died. Natalie was just thirteen then, and I don't remember that much about her."

They were both quiet again for the longest time before Dorian finally said, "You met her for dinner last night."

"Yes. We met her for dinner. Abby was so excited." Lorraine leaned her head back against the sofa. "I couldn't stop staring at her, Dorian. It was like having Tess there — Natalie looks just like her. Even their voices are similar. I'd noticed that on the phone the other day. But seeing her was something else. The way she moved. The color of her hair." Lorraine took another deep breath and closed her eyes again. "I think I freaked out a little."

"Did Abby notice the resemblance?"

"Not consciously, but she was drawn to Natalie in a way I'd never seen before. This woman had a profound effect on both of us."

Dorian waited for her to continue, and in the meantime remembered seeing the pictures of Tess on the mantel and having a good idea what Natalie must look like.

"Then just before we left the restaurant," Lorraine said, "Natalie admitted to having had this crush on me when she was a kid. I swear I don't remember seeing her more than two or three times. And there were always these horrible arguments when Tess was around her family."

She rubbed her eyes and pulled her hand down across her face. "*Then* Natalie told me she's a lesbian. By that time we were in the parking lot and Abby was chattering away and wanting Natalie to come over and see the pictures of the shipwreck, see her telescope, see the water guns and this and that. And all while Abby was going on about this stuff, I was standing there thinking I didn't want her to leave either. We had talked, but we *hadn't* talked, you know? So she followed us home, and the three of us were up half the night going through old photo albums of Tess and me. Then Abby as a baby. Then more pictures of Abby and me. Then the shipwreck photos. It got late, and I finally got Abby off to bed and settled down. And then I was suddenly back in my living room alone with her."

Lorraine's eyes brimmed slightly, but there weren't any tears yet. "Then I was alone with her," she whispered again.

Dorian knew in her heart that she had heard more than enough, but she couldn't stop the questions from flooding her thoughts, questions that were guaranteed to hurt her, guaranteed to break her heart all over again.

"Who made the first move?" Dorian finally asked.

Her voice sounded surprisingly normal and free of emotion.

"First move?" Lorraine repeated. "She made *all* the moves! I couldn't do anything but stand there and cry." Lorraine took another deep breath. "She was persistent and . . . thoughtful. I can't even explain what happened."

Jesus, Dorian thought as a lightning bolt of jealousy zapped her speechless. Dorian couldn't move as realization came to her in a flash of light. *I'm in love with her,* Dorian thought. *I'm in love with her and I've lost her already.*

"Damn it, Dorian," Lorraine said. "This is so bizarre."

"What happened this morning?" Dorian asked, as if someone else were making her talk, as if a ventriloquist were behind her making her mouth move and giving her words to say.

"This morning," Lorraine said. As she looked up at Dorian, the tears began rolling down Lorraine's face. "I think I was still in shock this morning. I don't even *remember* this morning. I'm seeing her again later tonight." Her eyes widened, and she seemed to try to get control of herself again. "It's painfully obvious why I'm doing this, Dorian, and I don't want to do it for these reasons. But I can't seem to stop myself."

"Does Natalie know what's going on with you?"

"I'm sure she does." Lorraine slowly sat forward on the sofa. "Anyway. I wanted to tell you all this up front. I'll admit to being confused and generally fucked up right now, but I wanted you to hear it from me and no one else." She got up from the sofa and went over to where Dorian was sitting. She put her hands on the arm of the chair and knelt beside it. "Tell me what you're thinking, Dorian. I know that under the circumstances this is a selfish and ludicrous thing to say, but I don't want to lose you over this."

Dorian closed her eyes and leaned back against the chair.

"I'm hurting you and I'm sorry."

"Don't worry about me," Dorian said in a hoarse whisper.

Lorraine stood up. "I need to pick up Abby. My parents tend to let her stay up too late." They walked to the door. Lorraine gave her a hug, which Dorian couldn't bring herself to return.

"I wish you would say something," Lorraine said. "Tell me I'm crazy . . . nuts . . . something, Dorian. Tell me *some*thing."

Dorian cleared her throat and said, "I think half the battle for you right now has to do with seeing Natalie for who she really is. She's not Tess."

Lorraine hugged her again and left.

Dorian tried to spend very little time thinking about Lorraine and Abby, but that did absolutely no good. She found herself crying at the strangest times and missing them both desperately. She tried to reason that she hadn't really spent enough time with them to be so attached, but she knew that wasn't true. And staying busy during the day didn't do a thing to alleviate the loneliness she felt at night before drifting off to sleep.

Dorian didn't know if a friendship with Lorraine

was possible any longer. Having a friend she was in love with didn't seem feasible.

Dorian had never wanted to compete with Tess's memory, even though that's what a true relationship with Lorraine would have entailed. A good deal of Lorraine's emotional existence was still tied up with Tess and her memory. *To have and to hold,* Dorian thought. The pain didn't seem to be lessening any.

It was Saturday night, and Dorian had been looking forward to unwinding at Ruffino's with her coworkers. She needed this distraction in the worst way. She parked next to Mia's car and found her coworkers at their usual table. Mia had saved a seat for her, and the group of ten graciously let her buy the next round of drinks.

At one end of the table the other two engineers were tossing golf jokes back and forth, brushing up in case they got a chance to tell one to the boss anytime soon.

"You two have no pride," Dorian said with a shake of her head.

"Sold that years ago," Will Garcia admitted.

They listened as Will's wife described how obsessed her husband had become over golf jokes lately. "He tells them in his sleep," she said.

"A good elbow in the ribs'll take care of that," Mia informed her.

"The voice of experience," Dorian noted.

Mia glanced over at her with a sly smile and a raised eyebrow. Before she could reply, Charlie asked Dorian how Rusty was doing. Everyone at the table burst out laughing at just the mention of his name. Rusty's and Dorian's mutual dislike for each other was no secret at Cohen Engineering.

"Are you on schedule?" Will asked.

"I'm always on schedule," Dorian reminded him as she held up her margarita in a minitoast. "Despite Rusty No-Butt Barnes."

The evening wore on, and people began to leave in pursuit of other Saturday night adventures, leaving only Dorian, Mia and Lawrence. Mia suggested they find a smaller table and order something to eat. They did and felt less conspicuous.

Lawrence waved away Mia's offer of a menu and checked his watch. "I'm picking up a friend at the airport later," he said. "Make sure I'm outta here in fifteen minutes, will you?"

Dorian ordered a salad and decaf coffee, remembering too late how bad Ruffino's coffee was. She listened as Mia and Lawrence talked about airport traffic and how Lawrence was going to get his friend's luggage into his tiny car. Dorian noticed the captivated look on Lawrence's face as he practically glowed from Mia's attention. Mia asked how his father was doing after his heart attack last year, and they talked about Lawrence's family and his parents' health. Dorian had always been impressed by Mia's uncanny ability with people. She could defuse uncomfortable situations from angry taxpayers to insolent city officials. She was a master at soothing rumpled feathers and finding reasonable solutions. Her comments were never direct or condescending, but instead she offered them as an afterthought or a mere suggestion. She was personable and amusing, and always knew the right thing to say.

Halfway through Dorian's salad, Mia reminded Lawrence that he needed to get to the airport, and Dorian was glad to see him go. The hour or so she and Mia usually spent together after the others departed Ruffino's always seemed to help Dorian unwind further. Mia had such a calming affect on her that all intrusions on this ritual were annoying. Dorian smiled and nodded toward the door Lawrence had just strolled out of.

"He's a bit infatuated with you."

Mia slowly dunked a fried mushroom into cream gravy and held the fork in front of her as she blew at the steam swirling around it. "Hmm. It's not like you to notice such things."

Surprised at this comment, Dorian raised an eyebrow and gave her a curious look. "What makes you say that?"

Mia smiled and shrugged. "You're always so focused on your work."

"I'm not as one-dimensional as you might think."

"All I'm saying is —"

"That I've got my head discretely elsewhere and the only things to get my attention are drainage ditches and highway construction," Dorian finished for her.

Mia's expression registered surprise before she speared another mushroom. "Obviously a touchy subject."

Dorian laughed. "Not really. I'm sorry. Please continue."

"I find it amusing that you can zero in on how someone like Lawrence reacts to me," Mia said, "but then you remain totally *clueless* when someone expresses a similar interest in you."

"What kind of interest?"

Mia smiled engagingly. "See what I mean? There's

someone in the office just as infatuated with you, Dorian Sadler. And from what I understand, that person has it pretty bad."

Dorian stopped poking the lettuce on her plate and set her fork down. She paled as she thought about each employee at Cohen Engineering—the surveyors, the drafters and the other two engineers. Most were married, some of the surveyors, like Lawrence, were still in school and were single, but Dorian had never gotten the impression that anyone had given her a second thought. It was a professional place to work. Even their Saturday nights at Ruffino's had structure of sorts.

"Clueless," Mia said, enunciating the word slowly. She chuckled in that low, throaty voice of hers, which just for a moment annoyed Dorian immensely.

"You're teasing me."

"Hardly. I'm dead serious."

"Really? Hmm. You aren't going to tell me who it is, are you?" Dorian said.

"Not on your life."

"And how long has it been since you first noticed something?"

"About a year now," Mia said. "Oh, and by the way. Phil and Diane are having a party in a few weeks," she said. "Everyone should get the word on Monday. You're the first to know."

Dorian was momentarily mesmerized by Mia's puckered glossy lips as they gently blew on another mushroom. She looked away and then cleared her throat before saying, "A party. What's the occasion?"

Phil and Diane's parties were legendary, and they

had several throughout the year, but here it was late April and not a holiday in sight.

"He likes to stay close to the troops," Mia said.

Dorian noticed how Mia's gray, silk shirt and her long, black hair complemented one another. Mia was an attractive woman, but Dorian refused to think about that. The next person she developed an interest in would be available in every sense of the word. Period. That hadn't been the case in either of her last two relationships. Gina had been married, and Lorraine . . . *Lorraine*, she thought. *Lorraine was even more married than Gina had ever hoped to be.*

"So," Mia said, interrupting her thoughts. "Here we are. You're miles away, Dorian. How are things with you?" She poked another steaming mushroom and pointed it at her. "I mean really."

Dorian smiled. "Things are okay."

Mia blew on the mushroom and studied her carefully. Their eyes met, and those slightly puckered lips meant only for the mushroom seemed to tease Dorian with their suggestiveness. The intensity of the look Mia gave her set off a new range of enlightenment for Dorian, and it occurred to her again how attractive Mia was.

"This is always my favorite part of happy hour at Ruffino's," Mia said. "Kicking back and eating things that are bad for me."

Dorian admitted that she liked this quiet time as well. "You always give me something to think about. You're very good at that, in fact."

They split the check and left the waitress a generous tip. "Such as?" Mia prompted.

"Such as where my head's been this last year," Dorian said. "Obviously the answer is 'firmly up my ass.' Am I right?"

Mia's sudden boisterous laughter caught Dorian by surprise and made her laugh as well.

"You're telling me that there's this little soap opera going on at work," Dorian continued. "A little soap opera that I'm in the middle of. Nothing there interests me. Trust me on that."

"I see."

They got in their cars and sped off into the night. As Dorian drove home she promised to be more alert to coworkers' actions, and maybe even put a little friendly pressure on Mia for more information. The last thing she needed was testosterone complications at the office, and she wanted no surprises.

Chapter Eleven

Dorian and Rusty were in the street inspecting the curb that she had strongly suggested his crew repair, and Dorian was relieved to see that everything looked good. The day always went much smoother when Rusty did what was expected of him.

"Nice job," she said. "I'll make sure the check's in the mail today." The only real control she had over him was the power of the dollar. Rusty didn't get paid unless everything met Dorian's specifications.

Later that afternoon before leaving the work site, Dorian sat in the back seat of the Geo Metro, her feet in crusty work boots firmly planted on the worn grass. She reached for her shoes on the floor just as a car pulled up beside her. Lorraine got out still dressed for work in a black skirt, a charcoal gray blouse and a matching black jacket. Even at the end of the day she managed to look fresh and ready for anything.

"Hi," Dorian said, surprised to see her. The fluttering in her heart confirmed any previous misconceptions about how she felt about this woman.

"I was hoping I'd find you here."

"So how's it going?" Dorian asked. She noticed that Lorraine didn't seem as stressed as she had the last time they'd met.

"You tell me," Lorraine said. She opened the door on the driver's side of the Geo and plopped down in the front seat. "Felicia still isn't speaking to me, and I'm in need of some advice."

"I give lousy advice," Dorian warned with a chuckle. "Let's make that perfectly clear right up front."

"I'll take that into consideration." Lorraine sighed. "This has to do with Natalie. Is that okay?"

Dorian cleared her throat and braced herself. Natalie was the *last* thing she wanted to hear about at the moment. "Sure," Dorian managed to say, and reminded herself again that Lorraine wasn't entirely aware of how she felt about her.

"Felicia says I've slept with the enemy," Lorraine said, getting right to the point. "And she thinks Natalie's family has sent her here to get in good with me."

Dorian knocked her boots together to try to get

122

some of the dried mud off. "It hasn't been that long ago that Tess's mother called about wanting custody of Abby," Dorian said.

"I know."

"And then a few days later Natalie shows up."

"I know that, too. Jesus. You sound like Felicia."

"It's not advice you want," Dorian said. "You're looking for someone who'll tell you that you're doing the right thing."

"*Now* you sound like Ethan."

Dorian laughed. "You're an intelligent woman, Lorraine. You don't need advice from anyone. You know the answers already."

"This is scary stuff, Dorian. What if Felicia's right? What if Natalie's here checking things out for her family?"

"Don't you think you'd be able to tell?"

"I don't know anymore."

Dorian took a deep breath and made it a point to sound concerned as well as indifferent. "What's your heart saying?" she asked, knowing full well that she didn't want to hear the answer.

"My heart?" Lorraine repeated and then sighed again. "My heart's in a coma. I'm not even sure it's there anymore." She looked at Dorian over the front seat and quietly said, "*Confused* doesn't even begin to describe me right now." She covered her glowing face with both hands and groaned her frustration. "Christ, Dorian. What am I gonna do? Natalie's trying to transfer here. She could be moving in the next few weeks."

Another spear seemed to pierce Dorian's chest. The

pain was incredibly intense, and she felt tears on the way. She cleared her throat again. "So you'll be living together?"

"No," Lorraine said. "Of course not." She folded her arms across her chest and began rocking back and forth. She glanced at Dorian over the seat again and gave her a questioning look. "Any words of wisdom you'd like to toss my way? I could use them right now."

The only thought in Dorian's head right then was that Lorraine wanted a life with someone else, and the pain of that realization gave her another jolt.

"Are you in love with her, or is it just sex?" Dorian asked.

"It's neither." Lorraine carelessly ran her fingers through her hair. "We only slept together that one time. I won't let her touch me again. It's too ... too ... weird." She closed her eyes and shivered. "Any suggestions?" Lorraine asked. "I need you, Dorian. Talk to me, damn it. Tell me what to do." She truly seemed to be at a loss.

"How does Natalie feel? Has she told you?"

"No." Lorraine looked at her over the seat again. "All she's said is that she doesn't care about the Tess thing. She wants me no matter who I'm thinking about when we make love." She covered her face with her hands again and mumbled, "This is just too weird."

Lorraine got out of the car and straightened her skirt and jacket. Dorian stood and set her boots on the floor in the back seat of the Geo.

"Just too weird," Lorraine said, and went around to the other side of her car. "Thanks for listening, Dorian. You've helped a lot."

Dorian felt terrible, like some dark, heavy cloud was hanging over her head, as if at any minute she would start to cry and never be able to stop. She watched as Lorraine drove away.

On the trip back to Dorian's office, she thought about her own life and where it was going. Career-wise, Dorian was just getting started. She planned to stay with Cohen Engineering until she got tired of building roads and drainage ditches. Even though Dorian loved that part of her job, she couldn't imagine doing it forever. Sometimes the bureaucracy got to be too much. That would surely burn her out long before anything else.

But her personal life was what she questioned. It was the only area where Dorian felt like a failure. Her relationship with Gina had been a mistake from the beginning, and, as a result, Dorian no longer trusted her instincts where women and relationships were concerned. Dorian could be demanding and rigid on a professional level, but she was shy and reserved when it came to her personal life. She seemed to run from hot to cold, as if her thermostat were on the blink.

As she slid between cool, clean sheets that night, she thought about Lorraine and Abby — a mother and daughter by chance — and how lucky they were to have each other. *And they were good for me,* she thought sadly as she drifted off to sleep. *So very, very good for me.*

Rain brought all of Cohen Engineering to the office on Friday, and it was almost like a reunion. Since Phil was in a bad mood because he couldn't play golf, everyone made it a point to stay clear of his office. Dorian could hear the *Golfing for Fun* video playing through the thin walls whenever she passed by Phil's door. They all knew the tape by heart, and occasionally someone could be seen mouthing the words as they went about their business in the office.

The thunder and lightning had stopped, but a slow, steady rain continued to fall throughout the morning. Everyone consumed coffee by the gallon, and Charlie and Will kept the surveyors and drafters entertained with their unending supply of golf jokes.

"So," Mia said as Dorian filled up her coffee mug from the fresh pot located behind Mia's desk. "Here we are."

"Yes. Here we are."

Mia handed over three messages in a neat little stack. "These are yours. All from Rusty complaining about the weather. He sounded like he was calling from a submarine."

"Has it rained that much?"

Mia smiled and extended her empty cup for Dorian to fill. "I imagine it's that cheap Kmart phone he has," she noted. "Have you thought any more about what we discussed the other night?"

Dorian looked at her blankly and then laughed. "You mean the office infatuation thing? No. Can't say as I have."

"And that's the difference between you and me," Mia said. "I would've spent every waking moment wondering who it is."

Dorian nodded toward the group of men surrounding a drafting table on the other side of the huge room. "If it's one of them, then what's the point?"

"But what if it's not?" Mia said, looking at her with those piercing, brown eyes.

Dorian returned the look and steadied her cup with both hands as the implication of Mia's question hit her full force. *She's either teasing you or else she's . . . omigod!* Dorian suddenly felt confused and a bit disoriented, gripping her cup so tightly that her hands began to ache.

"It's occurred to me that you need blatant," Mia said, never taking her eyes from Dorian's. "Coy and enticing hasn't worked with you, so I guess it's blatant or nothing."

Dorian set her cup down before she dropped it. *This isn't a tease . . .*

The phone on Mia's desk rang, and Mia reached to answer it without breaking eye contact with her. The look was smoldering and seductive, but Dorian was too surprised by this sudden turn of events to function.

"It's for you," Mia said, putting the caller on hold.

"I'll —" Dorian immediately heard the strain in her voice and then cleared her throat. "I'll get it at my desk." She left in a daze and returned to her office to take the call. She snapped into that formidable engineer mode as soon as she realized that the caller was Rusty. He started asking questions about the project they were working on, and Dorian assured him that she would keep them on schedule.

The call was brief, and afterward Dorian sat behind her desk and went over the last few non-work-related conversations she and Mia had engaged in. The one thing that stuck in her mind was Mia's reaction to Gina's visit the week before. Mia had been upset by it. Upset and . . .

"And jealous," Dorian said out loud. *Mia had been jealous.*

She let that sink in and leaned her head back against the chair. Dorian remembered their conversation at Ruffino's the other night where the word *infatuate* was tossed back and forth a few times. She could suddenly see things much more clearly now as she reached in her desk drawer and pulled out a *Webster's New World Dictionary*. Looking up the word *infatuate*, she found: "1. to make foolish; cause to lose sound judgment 2. To inspire with foolish or shallow love or affection."

"Lose sound judgment," Dorian said slowly. She closed the dictionary and put it back in the drawer. She couldn't imagine Mia losing anything, much less sound judgment. Dorian had never known a more organized, grounded or sane person than Mia Fontaine. This was so unreal. Mia was the object of *other* people's infatuations, so what was going on here?

There was a quick knock on her door, and then Mia came in with Dorian's coffee mug.

"You left this," she said, her tone a bit sharper than usual. "Are you going to hide in here all day now?" She set the mug down with a little flourish. "This blatant approach I've resorted to might've been a bad idea. I'm having second thoughts already."

With an effort, Dorian steadied her voice. "Second thoughts about telling me? Or second thoughts about . . ."

"Second thoughts about telling you," Mia said. "If it's a mistake, then so be it. I'll worry about that later." She moved Dorian's cup out of the way and put her hands on the desk as she leaned forward.

"I need to say this now, and I'll say it only once," Mia whispered. "I'm very attracted to you and I have been for several months. I'd like to discuss this with you at some point, but I'm not sure how, when, where or even *if* that's a good idea. And right now I've gone out on this limb about as far as I care to go at the moment." She stepped away from the desk and offered a weak smile. "Knowing you the way I do, I'm sure you'll process this information to death and agonize over every little detail while you're at it. Just keep in mind that Cohen Engineering is big enough for both of us no matter what happens next."

Dorian sat there stunned, having no idea what to say. Her heart was pounding, and for a moment she thought she might be dreaming.

"Rest assured that I won't mention any of this again," Mia said. "Business as usual." She turned to leave and stopped at the door. "By the way. Phil wants to see you in his office."

Dorian exhaled the deep breath she hadn't realized she'd been holding. Mia was gone, and Dorian suddenly felt exhausted. She was too shocked to be excited, but she at least had enough presence of mind to realize that something monumental had just occurred. In the beginning she had taken great pains to make sure her dealings with Mia remained professional and aboveboard. She realized now, however, that she had always sensed the attraction, but had managed to keep her mind on work and ignore the obvious.

She picked up her coffee cup and began thinking about Mia's announcement and what had just happened. *That took courage,* she thought. *Real courage.*

Leaving her coffee, she headed for Phil's office. On her way past Mia's desk Dorian stopped and said, "I'm still processing."

Mia's slow smile and the obvious relief on her face made Dorian's heart skip a beat.

"Take your time," Mia said.

Chapter Twelve

She went home that evening with more than enough to think about. Not only had Mia given a boost to Dorian's self-esteem, but Phil had informed her that he was giving her a promotion. Cohen Engineering had landed the contract for the I-10 expansion on the north side of San Antonio, a deal so big that Phil was making plans to give up golf for a while so that he could focus all his attention on this new project.

"And I want you working with me, Dorian. I need the best on this."

Phil promised her a raise and the keys to the new company car that was parked out front with less than seven miles on it. Dorian once again thought she might be dreaming.

"Let's take a ride and check it out," he said.

"Check out what?" Dorian asked as she followed him past Mia's desk at a leisurely pace. "I-10 or the new car?"

Phil laughed and tossed her the keys. "Both."

They'd spent hours out in the middle of traffic, shouting over the roar of chugging eighteen-wheelers and zooming cars. Phil's excitement was contagious, and Dorian lost complete track of time while they were gone. This would be a lengthy, lucrative project — one that Phil would tire of long before completion, she was sure. It occurred to Dorian at one point that eventually she might be in charge of the whole thing.

Later that evening she called her parents and shared her good news with them. Her father was more excited than even Dorian herself had been. Afterward she spent an hour answering the phone as word spread throughout the Sadler family. She was glad that her brothers were there for her, helping keep her mind off the fact that it was Friday night and that she was home alone. Each phone call was filled with new information about nieces and nephews, and kept her from thinking about Lorraine and Mia.

Dorian felt certain that being able to remain friends with Lorraine was a remote possibility. Other than Luke, Dorian didn't have a friend that she could wake up in the middle of the night for anything. The thought of not being able to call Lorraine depressed her, and she realized how impossible it would be to keep in touch with her under these circumstances. Dorian was in love with her and wasn't sure what to do about it.

So there she was, alone and needing to share her good news with someone other than her family. Dorian knew that being isolated and lonely wasn't good, and as she stretched out on her sofa and allowed herself time to think things over, she let thoughts of Mia enter her mind. There hadn't been a chance for Dorian to talk to her again. By the time she and Phil had returned to the office later that afternoon, everyone else had gone home for the day. Dorian had been disappointed about not seeing Mia again, but in a way she was glad to have more time to mull this situation over. Usually there wasn't an impulsive bone in Dorian's body, and she wanted everything clear in her head before she went anywhere else with this. Further on into the evening, however, she regretted not having Mia's telephone number, and at one point around nine-thirty Dorian considered driving back to the office to get it. The desperation and impulsiveness of that thought caught her completely off guard, and Dorian was forced to reevaluate how important Mia's revelation actually was to her.

By midnight, after having thought about things for several hours, she fell asleep, mentally exhausted, with Rusty Barnes giving her a one-finger salute as her last conscious thought.

* * * * *

The following morning was Saturday, and Luke woke her with a phone call and news that he had a brunch almost ready to start their day off. Dorian took a quick shower and went next door. She told him about Lorraine and Natalie, which did nothing but reinstate Dorian's sense of doom and gloom. From there they began analyzing the events of the previous day — the new company car, her promotion, and Mia's declaration — a process that improved Dorian's mood considerably.

"And all this time you didn't know what was going on with this Mia person?" Luke said incredulously.

"No," Dorian admitted. "I'm afraid not."

"Sometimes you're as dumb as stump water. How could you *not* know?" He poured them both more coffee. "Just don't go slobbering all over yourself because of this woman. She might very well be as straight as she looks." Luke dropped a sugar cube in his cup and gently stirred. "Just because she's attracted to you doesn't mean there's not a boyfriend around or a Roger-the-Husband somewhere in the picture. The two of them may have plans for you, if you know what I mean."

Dorian suppressed that little tinge of annoyance that Luke provoked sometimes.

"Mia's not like that."

"You don't know her well enough to know what she's like."

"Okay, okay," she said, dismissing him with a wave of her hand. He'd already put a damper on the little traces of a good mood she'd been able to muster. Dorian didn't need this dash of suspicion Luke was throwing on Mia's motives. The thing that made Mia's confession so appealing to Dorian was that it kept her from thinking about Lorraine and Abby every waking moment.

"And you're seeing her this evening?" Luke asked.

"Happy hour with some people from work."

"Good. It shouldn't take long to figure out where she's coming from. Hey, if things go well, then you can bring her back home tonight and —"

"Wait, wait, wait," Dorian said as she picked up a piece of bacon and bit off the end. "Home? Tonight?" She tossed her head back and laughed.

"You're damn skippy. Home. Tonight. What's wrong with that? She's interested and you're interested. Change the sheets and plug in an air freshener. *Boom.* You're ready."

Dorian shook her head, unable to imagine such a scenario. Mia. Home. In Dorian's apartment. Tonight. The mere thought made her laugh all over again.

"What's so funny?" Luke asked, irritated.

"I don't know. This is all so unreal to me."

"Tonight will take care of that. Eat up and let's go shopping. A new outfit will give you that edge you'll need."

Dorian spent thirty minutes laying out her new clothes, finally deciding on an old ensemble that consisted of crushed denim black pants, black boots, a long-sleeve white shirt and a thin black belt. Luke met her in the parking lot on his way back from the Dumpster, shaking his head with his hands on his hips.

"Where's the new stuff we spent all day shopping for? Those peach overalls were adorable on you!"

* * * * *

During the drive over to Ruffino's, Dorian was
nervous and kept checking her reflection in the
rearview mirror. Even though every hair was in its
correct place, she had to keep looking anyway. All day
she had been thinking about what she would say to
Mia tonight, and the thought of seeing her again outside of the office was quite a rush. There were several
things that she wanted to ask her before this went too
much farther, and hopefully tonight would be the
perfect time for it.

Dorian parked her Jeep and was disappointed that
Mia's car wasn't there yet. She glanced at her watch
and noted her usual fifteen-minute tardiness. Mia,
however, was never late for anything.

When Dorian went inside she spotted Lawrence,
Charlie and his wife Rose, and two of the drafters and
their wives at a table in the back. She sat down next
to Lawrence and ordered a gin and tonic.

Over the next five minutes several more people
arrived and borrowed chairs and crowded in closer.
They finally pushed two tables together and spread
out a little more. Every time a new person came in,
they asked where Mia was, as if the festivities couldn't
begin without her. Dorian glanced at her watch again
at seven-thirty just as Mia came in.

She wore a long blue flowery-print skirt and a
dark blue cotton blouse. Dorian felt such a sense of
relief at having her there, as if a light had finally
come on after days of darkness. The entire mood at
the table also changed, and Dorian realized how wired
she'd been all day waiting for this.

"Anyone sitting here?" Mia asked, indicating the

chair beside Dorian. She set her small purse down on the table and claimed to need an emergency Bloody Mary, which sent a hearty laugh around the circle.

"I've been saving my new golf joke till you got here," Charlie said.

Mia's bored expression set off another round of laughter. The waitress took more drink orders and momentarily distracted them. Mia sat down next to Dorian and hung the strap of her small purse over the back of the chair. As she did so she leaned closer to Dorian and said in a low voice, "I was hoping you'd make it tonight."

"I was early," Dorian said as she tried to ignore Mia's intoxicating perfume.

"You're never early to these things," Mia noted.

"And you're never late."

Mia laughed and tossed a shock of raven hair away from her eyes. "I couldn't decide what to wear. And I never have that problem. So what's the matter with us? You're early, I'm late, and I'm worried about the Clothes Police all of a sudden."

A wife of one of the drafters asked Mia a question about the company party that was to be at Phil and Diane's house the following Saturday. That spawned a long string of questions.

As Mia listened to a comment Charlie made, she leaned over to Dorian and whispered, "You look great tonight, by the way."

Dorian blushed and sipped her drink. "Thanks," she said, and was glad she hadn't worn the peach overalls. "Maybe we can get together later and talk."

"I'd like that," Mia said.

It ended up being an early evening as people left for other Saturday night plans. Several were going to a late movie together, while others were headed home. As they got ready to leave, Dorian suggested a coffee shop a few blocks away, and Mia followed her there.

They chose a table in a corner and placed their orders. Dorian had waited all day for this, and now that the time had arrived she wasn't quite sure what to do next.

Mia tossed her long hair over her shoulder and stirred cream into her coffee. She looked at Dorian as she held her cup close to her lips for a cautious sip.

Full, glossy lips, Dorian noted.

"What are you thinking?" Mia asked.

Dorian laughed and knew she was blushing again. "That's the problem. I think too much."

"So share some of those thoughts with me."

Dorian shrugged and made up her mind to get to the point.

"You say that you're attracted to me." The sentence seemed to hang in the air between them before Dorian continued. "I'm immensely flattered by that, and you won't find anyone more clueless than me when it comes to this sort of thing. But then *clueless* was your word describing me anyway, so you already know that."

They both laughed, which eased some of the tension.

"I find that endearing," Mia said.

Dorian tried to compose her thoughts and decipher her feelings all at the same time, but sorting through the uncertainty she felt seemed to be taking forever. "I need to know a little more about . . . how you got to this point."

With a puzzled expression, Mia asked, "Which point? Being attracted to you?"

"Yes."

Mia tilted her head and had a pensive look on her face. "How can I explain an attraction? It's just there. Nagging away, a constant reminder. I like you. I like you a *lot*. I find myself wanting to get to know you better. I think you're one of the most intriguing people I've ever known."

Dorian picked up her spoon and noticed that her hand was trembling. It was very easy to get distracted with words like *intriguing* and *attracted*, but this wasn't where Dorian wanted to go at the moment.

"How many women have you been attracted to?" Dorian asked.

"How many?" Mia repeated. "Why do you ask?"

"You're not a lesbian."

Mia slowly sipped her coffee again. "So you're into labels."

"I didn't say that."

"You didn't have to." Mia set her cup down. "I don't have any credentials to show you, Dorian. No one was there to issue me a membership card the first time I kissed a woman."

"Hmm. Yes. I see what you mean." Dorian nervously cleared her throat. "It's just that things are sort of complicated for me right now. I've made some bad choices where my personal life is concerned, and I'm not sure I've learned much from it. I'm not very good at this."

"We've all made bad choices," Mia said. "Most of mine were with men. If you're wondering if I'm gay, then my answer would have to be that I don't know. The only things I'm certain about are that I'm attracted to you and that I'd like to get to know you better." Mia glanced at her again. "Is this something you're interested in being a part of, or is this the last personal conversation we'll ever have?"

Dorian concentrated on her coffee as she contemplated her answer. "I'm emotionally unavailable right now," she said. She didn't want to get into this with Mia or with anyone. Her feelings for Lorraine were too raw, and dealing with the loss of both Lorraine and Abby was very painful. She couldn't see herself getting involved with anyone else right now.

"Emotionally unavailable," Mia said. She signaled the waiter for more coffee. "Please tell me you're not still in love with that Gina bitch."

Dorian was surprised at the viciousness in Mia's voice, but hearing Gina being referred to as a bitch also made Dorian laugh. "No. It's been over with Gina for a long time."

"But there's someone else," Mia said. She pushed her cup closer so the waiter could fill it. When he left she said, "You're not happy, Dorian. This other person isn't making you happy."

"It's complicated," Dorian said with a shrug. "She's in love with someone else, and I'm not ready to move on yet."

"You like torturing yourself. You want forever out of a relationship. On the other hand I'm at a place in my life where I'm more interested in just learning about me for a change."

Forever, Dorian thought. Another word that was becoming foreign to her. She picked up her spoon again and studied it for a moment before setting it back down. Hadn't Gina been interested in the same thing that Mia was talking about — exploring her sexuality and learning more about herself at Dorian's expense?

"You're thinking too much again," Mia said. "Come on. Out with it."

Dorian didn't know what to say. Suddenly she was very tired.

"Gina used you," Mia said, "and I would never do that. I'd like for us to spend some time together and get to know each other better. No strings or expectations. Is there anything wrong with that?"

Dorian tilted her head and arched her eyebrows. "No," she admitted.

"Good," Mia said with a laugh. "Then what are you doing tomorrow?"

After that small hurdle they spent another hour talking about the office and Dorian's promotion. And before the evening was over, Dorian agreed to pick her up for lunch on Sunday and then drive to the Hill Country for the Peach Festival in Fredricksburg.

Later, on her way home, Dorian realized that it had been a while since she'd had even one thought of Lorraine, Natalie or Abby. And for some reason that made her feel better.

Chapter Thirteen

"Tie your shoes," Lorraine said as she filled two bowls with corn flakes.

Abby shuffled to the table and sat down with a plop and that early-morning pout that always made Lorraine want to tease her into a better mood. The pout was just one of many things about Abby that reminded Lorraine of Tess. Abby would always be the most precious gift Tess had ever given her, and not a day went by that Lorraine didn't send a silent thank-you Tess's way.

Pouring milk into their bowls Lorraine said, "Shoe-strings," but was once again ignored. "Are you staying up later than you're supposed to? Reading my Nancy Drew books with the flashlight again?"

Abby rolled her eyes and picked up her spoon. Instead of answering the question, she asked one of her own. "Are you going with us today?"

"Nope," Lorraine said as she scanned the ingredients on the cereal box.

"How come you don't like Aunt Natalie anymore?"

Lowering the box Lorraine said, "Where'd you get that idea?" She had hoped that Abby hadn't noticed the strain between them whenever Natalie came by lately, but Lorraine knew how easily Abby picked up on such things.

"She never eats with us anymore or stays over. And you never go places with us when we ask you to."

"And that proves what?" Lorraine set the cereal box aside and renewed her interest in the corn flakes. "It's not me she wants to spend time with, kiddo." She pointed her spoon at her and said, "This way you get her complete attention. And we *all* know how you like attention. Did you tie those shoes yet?"

Abby groaned and hiked a sneakered foot up on the chair to tie her shoe just as the doorbell rang. Lorraine went to answer it and wondered if there would ever be a time when seeing Natalie wouldn't embarrass her. It was all she could do to look the attractive young woman in the eye as they exchanged generic niceties at the door.

"Have you had breakfast?" Lorraine asked. "Corn flakes are on the menu this morning."

"None for me. Thanks."

Natalie was dressed in tight jeans, brown soft-leather boots and a loose white T-shirt. Her light brown hair was stylishly cut to just below her collar, and at first glance she didn't appear to be too long out of high school, but in fact was a college graduate with a liberal arts degree.

Abby bounded out of the kitchen with her shoes neatly tied and that I'm-ready-to-go look that Lorraine immediately recognized. Natalie was taking her shopping for in-line skates. The discussion on whether or not Abby could have them had been going on for days now, with Lorraine's vote being the only dissenting one.

"You spring for the skates and I get stuck with the doctor bills when she breaks something," Lorraine had stated the first time the subject came up. "That doesn't sound like a good idea to me."

"She'll be fine," Natalie insisted. "Kids take to this stuff easily."

"Broken bones and tooth replacement are very expensive." Lorraine was certain she had won, but then her brother arrived with an offer to buy the headgear and knee and elbow padding that went with any in-line skate purchase. From there Lorraine was ferociously outnumbered, even though the final call had still been hers. Not wanting to sound like a stereotypical mother, she had eventually given in.

"Did you finish your breakfast?" Lorraine asked.

Eagerly nodding, Abby said, "Even drank my milk."

"Then go brush your teeth, wash your face and hands and bring back your hairbrush." Lorraine motioned toward the sofa, and Natalie sat down and gave her *the look* that Lorraine found so unnerving . . . *the look* that reminded her so much of Tess.

"Are you coming with us?" Natalie asked.

"No. I'm doing yard work today."

"You could do it later. Or even tomorrow." She crossed her long slender legs and laced her fingers together around her knee. "I could even come over tomorrow and help."

"Thanks anyway. I'll take care of it. I'm starting early while it's cool." Lorraine took the hairbrush Abby handed to her and positioned Abby between her knees. Abby's hair was blonde and thin, like Lorraine's had been at that age, and Lorraine noted with a smile how hard it was for Abby to be still for the two minutes it took to get her hair adequately brushed. When finished Lorraine kissed the top of her daughter's head, which was their usual signal that the hair torture was over. Tugging on Abby's hand, Lorraine asked what color skates she wanted.

"Don't know yet," Abby said as she scampered to the door.

"Ethan's meeting us for lunch before we pick out her helmet and padding," Natalie said. "You sure you won't join us?"

"Positive." Lorraine held the door open for them. "Have fun."

There was gas in the gas can, and the lawn mower started on the second try. *It doesn't get any better than this,* Lorraine thought with a smirk as she pushed the mower along the edge of the house in the backyard. In her mind the two most realistic euphemisms in *Murphy's Law for the Homeowner* were: "If it's grass-mowing day, then the gas can will be empty" and "If there's gas in the gas can, then the lawn mower won't start."

Dressed in gray sweatpants, a blue T-shirt, previously grass-stained sneakers and a blue bandanna to soak up sweat from her brow, Lorraine spent her Saturday morning making her yard look like everyone else's in the neighborhood. As she mowed the lawn and dodged a water hydrant and Abby's box turtle, Lorraine wondered how long it would take before she got over her embarrassment about sleeping with Natalie. For the first time in her life she was ashamed of her behavior; nothing had ever come close to this before. Lorraine had always been so careful about the women she took to bed. She liked being in control of that part of her life and insisted on making her own decisions, no matter how bad they were. And she made it a point to never sleep with a stranger.

But Natalie isn't exactly a stranger, she reminded herself again. Reliving that intense moment of weakness when Natalie kissed her nearly two weeks ago never failed to make Lorraine queasy. She still couldn't believe that she'd let it happen. In the dim light of the living room Natalie had looked so much like Tess then . . . her hair, the way she carried herself, the sound of her voice. Lorraine remembered feeling paralyzed at that moment, unable to speak or even breathe as Natalie moved closer to her. Soft lips touched Lorraine's, and then there was the perfume and what she imagined to be Tess's voice whispering in her ear.

Lorraine couldn't remember exactly when she

stopped thinking of Natalie as Natalie, Tess's little sister and Abby's aunt, and instead began thinking of her as Tess, the woman Lorraine had spent three wonderful years with, the love of her life, the keeper of her heart, the mother of her daughter. *What the hell happened?* she wondered. Was it that she had seen Natalie in semidarkness that evening? Seen her dressed the way Tess could've been dressed? Smelled the scent of Tess's perfume? Or was it that Natalie had reached for her so casually and touched her as though she'd done it a thousand times before.

Lorraine had no memory of them falling on the sofa or struggling out of clothes. All she could remember was the way her tears kept clouding her vision as Natalie made love to her. Lorraine cried all night and had wanted to hold her, to pull Natalie close and rock her gently as she buried her face in her hair. But Natalie had other plans and seemed determined to give Lorraine another type of night to remember.

Thinking back to that night two weeks ago, Lorraine truly believed that the whole thing, for her at least, had been nothing more than a mental breakdown of some sort — an honest case of temporary insanity.

Even during the first few moments of the dreaded morning after, Lorraine had still been in shock, but she realized soon after how outrageous her behavior had been. The resemblance had mostly existed in Lorraine's mind and had been nothing more than a silly trick that her imagination had played on her. *Where has my head been?* she kept asking herself over and over again.

Lorraine was quick to put the blame where it rightfully belonged. Nothing should've ever happened, and she had *allowed* it to happen anyway. But out of the handful of women Lorraine had shared her bed with since Tess had died, Natalie was the only one to bring about such a feeling of shame and betrayal. And lately Lorraine had spent many sleepless nights trying to figure out why. Was it because Natalie was Tess's little sister? Or was it because Natalie was willing to be someone else for her, and seemed to want her at any cost?

"That's sick," Lorraine mumbled as she moved the picnic table over so she could mow around it. "Sick, sick, sick."

There were things she wanted to ask Natalie, but she was waiting to see if her comfort zone with the young woman got any better. *Yeah, right,* Lorraine thought. *It won't get better until I spend some time with her.*

Thinking about Natalie tended to do nothing but depress her. Abby, Ethan, and Natalie had all noticed and commented on Lorraine's less-than-friendly manner toward Natalie during the last few days. *Just suck it up and get over it,* she thought wearily. *Invite her over for dinner tonight.* She sighed and yanked the lawn mower back before it chewed up Buster's tennis ball. *Just make sure Ethan's there the whole time.*

Fixing spaghetti reminded Lorraine of Dorian and those first few times she had come to dinner. It still surprised Lorraine how much she missed her; she liked thinking of Dorian as the only sane thing that had happened to her in a long time. Abby had finally stopped asking about Dorian once her Aunt Natalie had became a regular fixture in their lives, but Lorraine was acutely aware that she had bungled whatever chance she and Dorian had had together, whether as lovers or friends. With Natalie's unexpected whizzing onto the scene, Lorraine had known immediately that she had to be up-front with Dorian. Lorraine's life was complicated enough without the burden of juggling two lovers.

Lorraine heard the front door close just as she dropped the pasta into boiling water. A few seconds later Natalie leaned against the refrigerator beside her.

"How's she doing out there?" Lorraine asked as she gave the pasta a few swishes with a wooden spoon. Ethan and Natalie had spent most of the afternoon taking turns keeping Abby propped up on the skates.

"Better," Natalie said. "She's learning how to stop and slow herself down."

Lorraine shook her head. "Last time I peeked through the drapes, she looked like a broken ankle just begging to happen. I couldn't watch any more."

Natalie laughed. "She'll be fine. Kids are a lot more durable than you think."

"I'm her mother. That's not news to me. But the reason you know it so well is because you're not that far out of puberty yourself."

"Zing, zing," Natalie said dryly.

Lorraine laughed, but was still a little miffed that she'd been outnumbered on this skate thing.

"By the way, what are the chances of me being able to take Abby to South Carolina to see my family next weekend?" Natalie asked. "There's a reunion that I need to go back for."

Lorraine felt the tiny hairs on the back of her

neck stand at attention. "How does 'not a chance in hell' sound?" She had managed to say it without expressing the anger she felt.

"You could come with us," Natalie suggested.

Lorraine let her menacing look speak for itself. She wanted to keep her emotions and her suspicions in perspective, but her mind raced with questions. There were too many coincidences suddenly. The timing of the telephone call from Tess's mother vowing to sue for custody of Abby. Natalie showing up so soon afterward with sex and sympathy on her mind. Lorraine wondered how much preparation and forethought had actually gone into the seduction. Lorraine had been suppressing these and many more thoughts, giving Natalie the benefit of the doubt when questions about why she was here went unanswered. *And now there's a family reunion*, Lorraine thought *A weekend trip to South Carolina . . . she wants to take my kid out of state to visit those people . . . those people.* Lorraine cringed at the thought. *The same people who kicked Tess out in the street.*

"I'll get us tickets," Natalie said. "We can fly out on Friday and come back Sunday."

"I can't imagine me agreeing to much of anything where your family is concerned," Lorraine said. "So you'll be going back next weekend?"

"Just for the reunion. And I'd really like to take Abby with me."

Natalie sat down at the kitchen table and laced her fingers together, keeping her expression neutral, but maintaining eye contact. Lorraine watched her and wondered again how she could have ever mistaken this woman for Tess, or allowed herself to be so open to the suggestion that she could recapture something she'd lost so long ago. Lorraine was disappointed in herself for being so weak, and decided right then to do something about it.

"She's got cousins her age and other aunts and uncles that she's never met," Natalie said. "It'll be fun. I'll take —"

"Not this time," Lorraine said. "Maybe when she's older." She gave the steaming pot of pasta a few more swishes with the wooden spoon and then set it down on the counter. Lorraine turned back around and said, "And when Abby *does* finally meet your family, I'll be with her. You can count on that."

"Have you seen the shipwreck pictures?" Abby asked Natalie later that evening.

Lorraine, Ethan and Natalie laughed heartily at just the mention of the shipwreck pictures. Everyone had each picture memorized by now and could recite Abby's narrative already.

"Sure," Natalie said good-naturedly. "It's only been about two days since I've seen them."

Lorraine and Ethan cleared away the table while Abby and Natalie discovered the shipwreck pictures all over again. As Ethan scraped spaghetti off the plates he nodded toward the living room.

"I'm supposed to be convincing you to let Abby go to South Carolina this weekend. Why would she think I'd be on her side with this?"

"It gives the illusion of innocence," Lorraine said.

"You haven't changed your mind, have you?"

Lorraine gave him her best are-you-nuts look, then asked, "What do *you* think?"

They finished in the kitchen and went back out into the living room to find Abby and Natalie still on the sofa, discussing one picture in particular. Lorraine heard Dorian's name mentioned and went over to see which picture they were looking at.

"Dorian's a civilian engineer," Abby said with an air of authority. "She makes streets and sewer pipes and stuff."

"Civil," Lorraine said, correcting her. "She's a civil engineer. Not a civilian engineer."

"Civil engineer," Abby repeated. "She gave me a hard hat for my birthday. Wanna see it?"

"I've seen it," Natalie said.

Lorraine took the picture Abby held and looked at it more closely. This particular picture was the one Lorraine had taken of Dorian from across the cofferdam where she was talking to her brother. *What a beautiful woman she is,* Lorraine thought. It wasn't the first time she'd noticed how nice Dorian was to look at, but it was the second time that evening that she realized how very much she missed her. There were so many good things that went on inside of Lorraine when she thought about Dorian, and she couldn't believe how little it had taken to make the whole thing crumple. *You fucked that up royally, Rainey old girl,* she thought sadly. Lorraine gave the picture back to Abby and decided that it would be best not to think about it any more.

Chapter Fourteen

What Dorian found most amazing about Mia and
the time they spent together was how much fun they
had. During their Sunday jaunt to the Hill Country
for the Peach Festival they were where they wanted to
be in what seemed like record time, and conversation
flowed and laughter came easily. Mia talked about her
family and her ex-husband as though they were both
unsightly appendages waiting to be surgically removed.
Mia's parents, both retired and living in New York,

liked using her San Antonio home as a vacation stop during the winter months.

"I love my parents," Mia said as she cleaned her sunglasses on the tail of her sleeveless black denim shirt. "Don't get me wrong. And having them here once a year is great, but I'm always a little too excited when they start packing to leave."

Lunch in downtown Fredericksburg was at a quaint German restaurant. They had a table by the front window and enjoyed a glass of wine with their meal. Dorian answered questions about her own family and realized that several hours had gone by without a thought of Lorraine. And it occurred to her more than once how much she had missed having someone to talk to and do things with.

They did some shopping and sampled local festival delicacies at every opportunity — everything from peach ice cream to peach jerky. They split the cost of a bushel of fresh peaches and both swooned as the sweet fruity scent filled Dorian's Jeep.

It was already getting dark as they headed back home, and the conversation continued long after they arrived at Mia's house. They sorted through the shopping bags in the back seat, and then carried in the fruit.

"I can't believe we bought these," Dorian said as she set the basket down on Mia's kitchen counter. "What was I thinking? I probably eat maybe two peaches a year. Maybe."

"You give them away, Dorian. Neighbors. The mailman. Take them to the office. They won't last three days there." Mia placed her half of the bushel in the kitchen sink and then washed her hands. "Come over for dinner after work tomorrow," she suggested. "I'll make something peachy."

Dorian chuckled and then realized that Mia was serious. *She's inviting me over for dinner!*

"Well?" Mia said. "Yes or no? Do you have plans already?"

"Dinner sounds great," Dorian said, hoping that she didn't sound as surprised as she felt. "I'll bring some wine, or perhaps something . . . uh . . . peachy."

All the way home and on into the rest of the evening Dorian kept asking herself the same questions over and over again: *Are we dating? Are these little excursions we're going on actual dates?* Less than two days ago she had stated that she was emotionally unavailable, and Dorian wasn't quite sure how they had gotten this far so quickly. But Mia had seemed nonchalant about the dinner suggestion, so Dorian stopped worrying about it.

Monday morning as soon as Dorian entered the office she could smell peaches as well as fresh coffee. Phil arrived right behind her and kept Dorian in his office most of the morning. The two of them would be flying to Oklahoma City the next day to meet the contractor for the I-10 project. After this official meeting, Dorian would be spending a lot of time in Oklahoma laying the groundwork for future relations with the two companies. They would be stuck with each other for the duration of the eighteen-month project, so these first few meetings were vital to an amiable working relationship and ultimately the project's success. Phil wasn't happy with the contractor being from out of state, but there wasn't much he could do about it.

Back in her office later that afternoon, Dorian had worked through lunch and took time to help herself to a peach from the bowl of fruit on Mia's desk.

"You and Phil are on a seven-thirty flight in the morning," Mia said. "And you're booked on a six o'clock flight back tomorrow afternoon." She handed Dorian a slip of paper with the flight information on it. "Someone will be picking you up there, so you won't need a rental car. They were anxious to please." Mia gave her a lingering look and then said, "Dinner at my place tonight. Remember? Is seven okay?"

"Seven's fine," Dorian said. *Do I remember? Who is she kidding?*

Dorian rang Mia's doorbell and convinced herself that she wasn't nervous. She hadn't spent much time choosing her clothes for the evening, and she hadn't obsessed over selecting the peach brandy, even though she also brought along a bottle of her favorite wine. Dorian was determined to be casual about this, and so far everything was going as planned.

Mia answered the door in khaki pants, a lavender cotton shirt and sandals, and her hair was pulled back loosely with a matching lavender ribbon. She was stunning, and it wasn't until Dorian was standing in the living room that she began to notice how nervous she actually was. There had been moments during the day when Dorian wondered what she would do if Mia wanted more from her or even asked her to spend the night or something. Now Dorian wondered if she could handle the disappointment of Mia *not* asking her to stay.

"You look great," Dorian said as she handed over the wine and the brandy. "But then you always look great."

Mia smiled. "I'd return the compliment, but it would only embarrass you." She held up the wine bottle. "Let's start with this. I picked up a movie for later too in case we run out of things to talk about." She led the way to the kitchen and began working on uncorking the bottle. "On second thought, I don't care how much it embarrasses you, I have to say that you look quite fetching yourself, Ms. Sadler."

Dorian cleared her throat and knew that she was blushing already. "Thanks." Glancing around the kitchen she asked, "What smells so good?"

"Probably the cobbler. Dinner's about twenty minutes away from being ready. Let's go in the living room and chill for a few."

Dorian chose to sit in the recliner, and Mia stretched out on the sofa. The living room was spacious with what looked like new white furniture — two recliners, a sofa and a love seat. The carpet was also white, and a low coffee table with an impressive glass top took up a nice bit of space.

They talked about how much time Dorian would be spending out of town during the next few weeks and about how strange it had been lately to have Phil in the office so much.

"He has a lot of respect for you," Mia said. "I hope you realize that he won't keep this pace up forever. He wants to get you settled in on this project so he can resume his normal life again."

Dorian smiled knowingly and sipped her wine. "I know what he's up to."

A buzzer went off in the kitchen, and five minutes later they were at the table eating. "Save room for peach cobbler and ice cream," Mia said.

They finished the wine and lingered over dessert, but there was nothing to suggest that anything more than two friends having dinner was going on. Office-related chatter overshadowed whatever intimate, personal conversation could've been. Dorian and Mia were careful what they chose to talk about even though the wine helped loosen Dorian up a little. When they returned to the living room later to watch the movie, they took turns sleeping through it, and when it was finally over, much to Dorian's embarrassment, Mia had to wake her up while the movie was rewinding.

"Who's taking you to the airport in the morning?" Mia asked as she stretched and yawned. It was only ten-thirty, but they were both still sleepy from their naps.

"I'm picking Phil up at six." Dorian checked her watch. "I need to get going. Hey, dinner was wonderful." She stretched again and laughed. "And the movie was just what I needed."

They made plans to meet for dinner Wednesday evening, and on her way home Dorian felt better than she had in weeks.

Dorian spent a good portion of her Saturday taking care of several things for the I-10 project. She finally left the office early that afternoon so she could get some rest before Phil and Diane's party that night. Mia was busy helping Diane with last-minutes details, so Dorian hadn't seen her or talked to her all day. They'd had dinner together every night that week, and it felt strange not having Mia available when Dorian wanted her to be.

During their time together lately, Mia and Dorian talked a lot about work and the employees at the Oklahoma office that they were dealing with on a daily basis. Their evenings together frequently ended with the two of them relaxing over dinner somewhere and then talking for another hour out in the restaurant's parking lot next to their cars. Dorian's work schedule was too unpredictable to make any real plans, so spontaneous dinner arrangements were working well for them. By Saturday evening, Dorian was anxious to see Mia again, even though it had been less than twenty-four hours since they'd parted at a Shoney's restaurant near the office.

Dorian pulled her Jeep up in front of Phil's house; she could hear laughter coming from the backyard as soon as she opened her door. She went in through a gate at the side of the house and found eight people in the pool already, four on each side of a small net stretched across its center. She waved to coworkers and their spouses, and found Phil on the other side of the huge yard tending to a smoking grill. Lawrence and Charlie were beside him talking, each with a drink in hand, no doubt exchanging golfing tips. ZZ Top was blaring from speakers cleverly disguised as stones around the pool, and laughter came from all areas throughout the yard.

Charlie handed Dorian a wine cooler from an ice chest and congratulated her again on her promotion.

"Thanks," she said, and glanced around the familiar faces, checking to see if she'd somehow overlooked Mia.

Someone called Dorian's name and pointed to an empty chair on the deck. It was Diane, Phil's wife and the hostess for the party. Diane moved lawn furniture around until there was room for one more person.

"We've got water polo, horseshoes and a vicious pool tournament going on in the den," Diane said. "And extra swimsuits if you didn't bring one." She gave Dorian a hug. Diane was a petite blonde in her mid-thirties. She and Phil, who didn't have any children, spent most of their time on the golf course. "Phil says you're kicking butt in Oklahoma City," Diane said with that boisterous laugh of hers. "How do you feel about that group up there?"

Dorian shrugged. It didn't surprise her that Diane knew so much about what was going on at Cohen Engineering. Phil seemed to share everything with his wife, and Dorian often wondered how much influence Diane Cohen had had in Dorian's initial hiring.

"They seem to know what they're doing," Dorian said. "And that's basically all that matters."

Even though Mia had made it very clear to the coordinators for the Oklahoma staff that Dorian was the engineer they'd be dealing with, the contractors had attempted to treat her merely as Phil's assistant during the meeting. But it was Dorian who gave the presentation and answered the majority of their questions. Phil only spoke up when questions were asked of him directly. Dorian could have easily handled the meeting on her own, but she and Phil both knew that his presence during the first few meetings was nothing more than a confidence-building exercise. Engineers and contractors seldom maintained any semblance of respect for each other and their talents. Each project started out full of hope for a smooth, day-to-day working relationship, but that sense of cohesiveness and the illusion of being able to work together as a team seldom lasted through a project's completion. There were two things that would keep them off schedule — bad weather and contractor error and incompetence. It was a fact of life, something Dorian dealt with every day. She knew she would have to prove herself over and over again. As it was, contractors thought that engineers were grossly overpaid, and a female engineer would border on ridiculous in their eyes. But again, that was something Dorian encountered every day, and the vibes she'd received in Oklahoma City were no different from the ones she'd experienced in her own hometown. Dorian did, however, choose not to share the rough spots during the meeting with Mia, but it was obvious that Phil had shared them with Diane.

"Where's Mia?" Dorian asked.

"Playing pool, I think," Diane said. "At least that's where she was earlier. Let's go see who's winning."

Dorian followed Diane into the house, where more voices could be heard and ZZ Top sounded more technically enhanced and CDish and less canned.

Once they reached the den, they found ten people standing around the pool table. Mia held a pool stick in one hand and a margarita in the other. She smiled and winked at Dorian, which sent a tiny current of energy racing through Dorian's body.

"Who's winning?" Diane asked. As everyone turned to see who had spoken, they all greeted Dorian.

"They are," Will said, "but it's still early. Who wants to play the winner? I think Mia and I've whupped everybody here already."

"How about it, Dorian?" Diane asked. "You and I can play the winners."

"How fair would that be?" Dorian asked. "It's your table."

"No advantage whatsoever," Diane said. "Believe me. I'm a lousy pool player. It should be a quick game." Her easy laughter made everyone else laugh too.

Mia and Will won the game and got a little cocky in their latest victory. It was their fourth straight win.

As Will racked the balls, Mia leaned over Dorian's shoulder and whispered, "The loser buys dinner tomorrow night."

Dorian smiled. "Then get ready to pick up the check."

"Ooohhh," Mia said with a delightful chuckle. "Listen to you."

Dorian selected a pool stick from the rack and slowly chalked the tip. She felt Mia's eyes on her and liked having them there. Mia looked fabulous in white shorts, a tangerine cotton shirt and white sandals. Her long, black hair was straight and glossy and flowed down her back. She was beautiful and, as always, had most of the room's attention.

"Where's that little square thing I'm supposed to use?" Diane asked innocently.

"It's chalk," Dorian said. "And it goes on this end of your pool stick." Dorian demonstrated how to properly apply it. "And you use it after every shot, okay?"

"*Every* shot?" Mia said. "Really?"

"Really. *Every* shot," Dorian confirmed. "Who breaks?"

"You do," Will said as he finished racking.

Dorian lined up the cue ball and sent the triangular clump of balls at the other end scattering in all directions. Three solid-color balls fell into the pockets. The spectators applauded enthusiastically, and Diane, who giggled delightedly, kept elbowing people and saying, "That's my partner. Did you see that shot?"

"Three ball in the corner pocket," Dorian said as she chalked the end of her pool stick again. There was a smattering of laughter throughout the crowd, and Dorian tried to remain pensive and serious when she heard Will mumble, "Oh, puleeze," under his breath.

She tapped the three ball into the corner pocket as promised and then proceeded to run the table, calling each shot after careful consideration of the table's layout. Dorian banked the eight ball across the table and graciously returned Diane's jubilant hug to a roomful of laughter and applause.

"We've been hustled," Will said with a laugh. "Where'd you learn to shoot pool like that?"

Dorian returned her stick to the rack and set the chalk cube down. "Four brothers and a pool table in the basement during my formative years." She noticed Mia at the end of the table watching her with new intensity. Mia smiled and shook her head as she came closer.

"You never stop amazing me," she said. "What other secrets do you have?"

"That's it," Dorian said. "Now you know everything there is to know about me."

"Oh, I doubt that." Mia reached around her and placed her pool stick on the rack.

"Ruffino's tomorrow evening at six," Dorian said. "And I believe you're buying, if I'm not mistaken."

As the evening continued Dorian became more aware of Mia and her intense looks across the room. Dorian liked Mia's laughter and her ability to be the center of attention in such a nonthreatening way. It was that Mia Fontaine mystique again.

Diane, Mia, Dorian, and Charlie's wife, Rose, were in the kitchen preparing a few last-minute menu items. Diane asked Mia to use the step ladder to reach a platter in a seldom-used cabinet over the refrigerator. Dorian was busy at the sink washing lettuce when she caught a glimpse of Mia's tanned, shapely legs climbing the small ladder to retrieve the platter. The white shorts with sharp creases and those legs that seemed to go on forever were right there at eye level. Dorian was speechless and totally immobile at that moment. She couldn't remember where she was or what she was doing there.

As Mia descended the ladder, her eyes met Dorian's, and something new and exciting happened between them. The look was smoldering and intense. Lust and passion were in the air, thick and compelling. Dorian knew without a doubt that they would make love later that evening, and it would take tremendous self-control on her part to wait until the party was over.

Chapter Fifteen

Dorian had refrained from consuming any more alcohol and noticed that Mia had done the same. It was after midnight and the party was beginning to wind down, but several people were still not quite ready to call it a night.

Even though Dorian and Mia had been pulled in different directions during most of the evening, they maintained a constant awareness of each other. Anyone could have easily interpreted their smiles and smoldering looks, but by then neither cared what anyone else thought. Dorian felt giddy and eager and tried thinking of a way to get Mia alone somewhere for just a few minutes, but that idea wasn't materializing. Phil and Charlie kept Dorian occupied near the pool with questions about the I-10 project, while Dorian noticed that Lawrence and one of the drafters were attempting to keep Mia entertained on the deck near the back door.

Earlier in the evening when Dorian and Mia were helping bring the food outside, Mia had asked her to come over to her house later. "We'll eat some peaches or something."

Eat some peaches, Dorian thought. *Sheesh. Your peaches may never be safe with me again, Ms. Fontaine.*

Dorian nodded at a comment Charlie made and then tried to concentrate on what Phil was saying, but her thoughts weren't with them at all. She imagined herself arriving at Mia's house later and the two of them sitting on Mia's sofa. They'd have some wine and discuss the party. They'd be sitting close together, and Dorian would eventually lean over and kiss her.

And that thought alone made her look at her watch and wish that the party were over already.

"Phil, honey," Diane said as she came up behind them and hooked her arm through his. "Did Dorian tell you that we won the pool tournament?" She threw her blonde head back and laughed, making it obvious that she'd spent a lot of time at the margarita machine during the evening.

Dorian looked up and saw Mia coming toward them with her entourage following close behind. *God, she looks good,* Dorian thought, and she wouldn't have been surprised in the least to know that others were thinking the same thing.

Dorian listened as Mia thanked Phil and Diane for a wonderful party, and as she turned to leave, Mia leaned closer to Dorian and said, "My place soon. Don't forget."

Forget? Dorian thought. *Who's she kidding? How could I forget?*

Dorian watched her make her way back across the yard, waving at coworkers and their spouses. Apparently Lawrence had taken it upon himself to escort Mia to her car. Dorian in turn set the wheels in motion to leave as well. She knew it would be easier for her since she could always claim to have work to do, which was unfortunately true.

Ten minutes later Dorian was through the back gate and headed toward her Jeep when she saw Lawrence and Mia talking by Mia's car. Dorian had expected Mia to be nearly home by now. She waved at them and got in her vehicle, and, much to Dorian's relief, Mia then got in her own car and pulled out, speeding like a demon.

Dorian searched the airways for music to match her mood on the way, and she finally just popped in a Lauren Wood CD and hummed along. She decided that the party had been good for her. Dorian liked knowing that Mia wanted her. At the same time, she liked knowing that others wanted Mia.

White sofa, wine, party gossip and kiss, she thought. *In that order.*

As Dorian parked behind Mia's car in the driveway, she wondered what kissing her would be like. And Dorian was more than ready to find out. Once again she thought of them sitting on the white sofa, drinking wine and talking about the party before they got down to anything as intimate as their first kiss.

Dorian rang the doorbell and was surprised when Mia answered it immediately. The second the door opened, Mia began unbuttoning her shirt and then unzipped her shorts in what seemed like slow motion. Lust was in her eyes, and neither of them spoke as Dorian closed the door and stood there like a mannequin, soaking up the sight of her. The white sofa, the wine, the party gossip — it was all forgotten, obliterated from Dorian's mind as Mia stepped into her arms and kissed her.

Dorian felt a roller coaster race through her body, looping and diving in her stomach as Mia's lips met hers. The kiss was deep and exhilarating, and Mia was making it very clear that she knew what she wanted and knew how to get it. Dorian was trembling, but just as eager to touch and excite as Mia was. Their kiss became hot and feral as Dorian slipped her tongue in Mia's mouth and pulled the shirttail from her shorts. Dorian pushed Mia's shirt off her shoulders before starting on her bra.

Mia's hands moved to the back of Dorian's neck as she continued kissing her. After a moment she pulled her mouth away and began kissing Dorian's throat.

"God, I've wanted this for so long," Mia said in a husky whisper.

Dorian added Mia's bra to the pile of clothes on the floor and filled her hands with Mia's warm, ample breasts.

"This way," Mia said, and she kissed her again with such passion that Dorian felt weak in the knees. Mia, who was now naked, took Dorian's hand, led the way to a bedroom across the hall and pulled Dorian down on the bed with her. They rolled around in a kissing frenzy, with Dorian eventually ending up on top but still fully clothed. Mia wrapped her legs around Dorian's back and began writhing against her. Dorian captured a jiggling breast with her mouth and liked the way Mia's nipples grew harder with each flick of her tongue.

"Suck my clit," Mia said in that hushed, throaty voice. "Please. Suck me hard." She grabbed Dorian's head and pushed her down between her legs. "Suck me, baby. Please. Suck me hard."

Mia's hands were on the back of Dorian's head again, and her legs were spread wide. The moment Dorian's mouth touched her, Mia began to move and grind herself against Dorian's face.

"Suck me!" she hissed. "Suck me, suck me, suck me. Oh god yes, yes, yes. Like that. Yes. Harder. Suck me harder!"

Dorian did as she was told and was rewarded not long afterward with a screaming, bucking, crazy woman fucking her face as though she were possessed. Dorian grabbed Mia's thighs and hung on for the ride. When it was finally over Mia gripped Dorian's hair in both hands and held her head there in place as she moved her hips back and forth to wring the last bit of pleasure and sensation from Dorian's mouth. Mia was trembling and drenched with sweat from the excursion, her breathing a series of short gasps.

When Mia finally allowed Dorian to come up for air, she lay back on the bed, her black hair fanned out behind her, with the most peaceful, satisfied expression on her lovely face. She was beautiful, hot, and sexy.

"Three minutes," Mia said weakly as she held up three fingers. "I'll be ready in three minutes. Then I want you to do me again, okay?"

Again? Dorian thought, surprised but happy. *This? Again? My god. Again?*

The next morning Dorian woke up to the smell of bacon frying. She was in the middle of Mia's bed and still had her clothes on. She'd never gotten undressed the night before, and, in fact, still had her shoes on.

She gingerly ran her tongue over her swollen lips and realized that they were very sore. She didn't remember how many times she'd made love to Mia last night. Shaking her groggy head, Dorian rolled over on her back. She had lost count after four, and each time Mia came she'd hold up the same three fingers and say, "Three minutes. I'll be ready again in three minutes."

Sleeping with Mia was without a doubt the strangest experience Dorian had ever had in bed. Mia liked kissing and being kissed and having her breasts touched, but only as a preamble to Dorian's mouth on her. And every time Dorian did it, Mia would come. And every time Mia came, she would scream and thrash around the bed as though someone were after her with a sharp stick. It was an amazing thing to be a part of, and after a while Dorian began worrying about her. Would Mia have a heart attack? Could someone die from such intense stimulation? And then again, a while later, Dorian began worrying about herself! After one rambunctious bucking session, Dorian tasted blood on her lip, but by then she was too caught up in it, too much a part of the pleasure process.

"Hi, sleepy head," Mia said as she came into the room. "I'm making breakfast." Dressed in a long white robe, she sat on the edge of the bed. "Here's a cool rag for your mouth. I'm sorry I hurt you last night."

Dorian took the rag and dabbed her bruised and swollen lips. Mia smiled down at her and moved the hair away from Dorian's eyes with a gentle sweeping motion on her forehead.

"You were so good with me last night," Mia whispered. "You never questioned me. You just went with it. God, if you only knew how good it was."

"I was here," Dorian said, the sleep still clinging to her voice. "I heard you. I felt you." She propped herself up on her elbows and smiled. "I know exactly how good it was for you."

"Yes," Mia said with a delighted laugh. "Maybe you do. And now I plan to make it just as good for you." She ran her fingers through the front of Dorian's hair again. "Would you like breakfast first? Breakfast before pleasure?"

"My lip hurts," Dorian said. Being kissed right then would no doubt be painful, and she couldn't imagine someone making love to her and not kissing her.

"I'll be careful," Mia said. She kissed Dorian's forehead and whispered, "I plan on taking very good care of that mouth of yours."

Making love with Mia was at times a bit frustrating, but Dorian was getting used to it. They had a routine of sorts, which consisted of Dorian making love to her until exhaustion took over and then Mia reciprocating the next morning. The heightened stimulation Mia received when Dorian made love to her caused Mia to be very sore for several days afterward, and during that recovery period there was no sexual activity at all between them. And Dorian's attempts to introduce different positions and techniques didn't go over very well either.

"I can come other ways," Mia said one night, "I just like this way best."

And who was Dorian to question what someone else found pleasurable? By the time Mia's body had recovered enough to give it another go, Dorian's lip was usually healed. And the frequent trips to Oklahoma City helped some too since Dorian was having to spend more time out of town.

But what Dorian found the most disturbing was Mia's attitude about her own sexuality. She was adamant about not being called a lesbian, and she didn't like Dorian using the word to describe herself. She believed that such labels were unnecessary and did more harm than good. Dorian, on the other hand, felt very comfortable using words like *lesbian*, *queer* and *dyke*. There was no compromise for them with this. They had complete opposite opinions on this subject.

"What's wrong with calling it what it is?" Dorian asked over dinner one night. "I sleep with women. My focus is women. I identify with women. I'm proud to be a lesbian. There's nothing wrong with it."

And the one time Dorian mentioned the word *bisexual*, Mia stopped eating dinner altogether and was so angry that she refused to talk the rest of the night.

172

Dorian apologized for upsetting her and went home, but she continued thinking about it all night. She wasn't sure what bothered her the most, the fact that Mia was willing to sleep with her but was ashamed of what Dorian was, or the fact that Mia was unwilling to put a name to what she herself was doing and feeling. Dorian *needed* a label for her lover if she was to continue on with this aspect of their relationship. As petty and childish as it sounded, she had to hear Mia describe her sexuality in some term that Dorian was familiar with. She had to have a word for it, a word of Mia's choosing. Once the word was out in the open, then Dorian would deal with the consequences. Gina and her betrayal had made labels a necessity in Dorian's life, and she refused to apologize for it any longer. If choices had to be made, then Dorian was willing to make them and risk everything for what was right for her.

The next time they had dinner, Dorian refused to let the subject drop. "I need to be involved with a lesbian," she stated flatly. "I want to worry about the women who look at you a certain way. I know what they're thinking and what they want. I can deal with that. I *understand* that. But I can't handle not knowing where your head's at with this."

Dorian could see that glazed look spread across Mia's face. She was getting angry again, but Dorian didn't let that stop her.

"I refuse to spend another *second* of my life wondering if some man is turning your head. If you need something a little different," Dorian said. She remembered Mia and Lawrence talking in the street after Phil's party. Other than good-bye, what else had been said? "I *know* this is my problem," Dorian continued. "I'm very aware of that. But it's serious to me, and I've chosen not to have these concerns in my life any longer."

Through clenched teeth, Mia said, "You're the only one I want to sleep with."

"For now."

Mia wadded up her napkin and threw it on the table. "For now! Okay? For now!" She picked up her wineglass and took a gulp. "It's that Gina bitch. She did this to you."

"It doesn't matter who did what," Dorian said wearily. Neither of them was hungry any longer. They went into the living room and sat on the sofa, both stretched out on opposite ends facing each other.

"You're the only one I want to sleep with," Mia said again in a calm, reasonable voice. "That has to count for something."

"It does."

"But it's not enough."

"No," Dorian admitted. "It's not enough. The woman I sleep with needs to be a lesbian. I'm sorry."

Mia sipped her wine and set her glass down on the coffee table. "So what happens now? Do we become just friends?" She shook her head and shuddered at the thought. "I don't like that idea. I'd always want more from you. Maybe we could be friends who sleep together. What's the term they use now?" Mia thought for a moment and then said, *"Fuck buddies?"*

They both burst out laughing. Mia Fontaine was *not* fuck-buddy material.

Chapter Sixteen

Dorian and Mia eventually agreed that they made better friends than lovers. They enjoyed each other's company and had dinner together whenever Dorian was in town; the I-10 project was keeping them both very busy. Dorian even had a standing reservation at a downtown hotel in Oklahoma City.

When Dorian was in San Antonio and she and Mia were together at the office, it was basically business as usual, but occasionally Mia would find Dorian alone and then say something suggestive or kiss her lightly on the lips. They hadn't slept together since the "fuck-buddy" discussion several weeks before, and they both seemed to have adjusted quite nicely to this new phase in their relationship. Dorian liked the closeness and humor they shared, and she found herself respecting Mia's stand on *not* labeling her sexuality. Mia was Mia. You could take her or leave her. It didn't really matter to her.

"You've got the weekend off," Mia said one Thursday night as she opened the warm pizza box. "Let's do something tomorrow. Go somewhere."

Dorian looked at her with an arched eyebrow. "All I *do* is go. *Not* going sounds much more appealing to me."

"Then let's do a movie Saturday night. There has to be something we'll want to see."

Mia was the only person Dorian knew who ate pizza with a knife and fork. She seemed to almost have an aversion to touching it. The table was set and the pizza presented on a crystal platter. Dorian often thought of ways to help her loosen up a little.

"Then afterward," Mia said, "maybe we could go to that billiards place on San Pedro and you can teach me how to play pool." She smiled innocently. "You promised you'd teach me. Remember? Ladies play free. Any time, any day."

"Hmm," Dorian said. "All the more reason not to go there, I'd think. But we can if you want to. I did promise."

On Friday night Mia picked her up at the airport and they went directly to the restaurant where they were to meet Luke and Cedric for dinner. Cedric got called away on an emergency halfway through his meal, and Dorian and Mia were stuck with a sulking Luke for company.

"You knew he was a doctor when you married him," Dorian said. "Stop being such a bitch."

Four jumbo margaritas later, Luke was a sulking, drunken bitch. Mia helped Dorian get him home.

"Did you like it?" Dorian asked as they followed the crowd out of the movie theater Saturday afternoon. She already knew the answer, but she wanted to hear Mia admit it.

"Yes, damn it. I liked it. Okay?"

Dorian laughed and loved teasing her this way. While they were going over the list of movies in the paper earlier, Dorian couldn't believe that *Titanic* was still playing. It had just been released on video, and Mia had argued that they could rent it any time they wanted to.

"Have you seen it?" Dorian asked.

"No."

"Then I think it'll be better on the big screen."

"We already know what happens," Mia argued. "They build a huge ship, it hits an iceberg, the ship sinks and people die. What's the big deal? Been there, done that, sold the T-shirt in a yard sale already, for crissakes."

Once they were outside in the late afternoon sunshine, the crowd began to thin as moviegoers straggled to their cars or the ticket counter. A young voice squealed her name, and Dorian turned to find Lorraine and Abby walking toward them.

"Abby! How are you!" Dorian was down on one knee giving her a hug. "You're growing like a weed, kid." She stood up again and smiled at Lorraine. It was great seeing them.

"She still smells good, Rainey," Abby said as she looked up at Lorraine and took her hand.

Lorraine laughed and introduced herself to Mia. Dorian pointed to Abby and then said to Mia, "Hard-hat birthday present. Remember?"

"Oh, so *you're* the one."

Lorraine smiled. "She still wears it around the house. And we've had to have several long talks about being a nuisance with the shipwreck pictures." She looked down at Abby for confirmation. "Haven't we?"

Abby shrugged and scuffed the toe of her shoe on the sidewalk. But then in the next moment her blue eyes lit up again. "We're gettin' hot dogs at Coney's. Can you come with us?"

"I'm sure Dorian has other plans already," Lorraine said.

"A hot dog sounds pretty good to me," Mia said. She glanced over at Dorian, who nodded in agreement. They decided to meet at the Coney's down the street.

"I thought you wanted to play pool," Dorian said once they were in her Jeep and off into traffic.

"How long does it take to eat a hot dog?" Mia asked. She lifted the mass of hair off her neck to help her cool down a little. "You and Lorraine have been lovers, haven't you?"

"Yes," Dorian said. "Briefly."

"Is she the one you were in love with?"

"Does it matter?" Dorian didn't like talking about this. Too much old baggage was involved, baggage that she had hoped had already been unpacked.

"Just asking," Mia said. She let go of her hair, which fell in place down her back. "You really *are* clueless about these things, aren't you?"

"Now what?"

"That woman's crazy about you."

Dorian laughed. "I don't think so."

"Clueless. You're absolutely clueless."

Dorian just looked at her.

"And the daughter," Mia said. "What's her name? Abby? She adores you."

"Why all this sudden interest in my love life . . . or lack of, as the case may be."

"I'm telling you, this woman's crazy about you. I can see it in her eyes. The way she looks at you."

"She's got a new girlfriend."

"So where is she? I didn't see any girlfriend. And women with new girlfriends don't look at other women the way she was looking at you."

Exasperated, Dorian said, "This discussion is over."

"We'll see," Mia said smugly before mumbling the word *clueless* one more time.

Abby waved excitedly as Mia and Dorian came up the sidewalk beside the restaurant. They got a booth right away. Abby and Lorraine sat on one side and Mia and Dorian on the other.

"Do you like those little crane machines?" Mia asked Abby.

Lorraine laughed. "She can go through a roll of quarters in under two minutes."

"Let's see what we can get," Mia said as she followed Abby to the crane machine full of stuffed animals.

"Mia's nice," Lorraine said after a moment. "How long have you been seeing her?"

"We're just friends. We work together." Dorian set her menu aside and asked the question she wasn't sure she wanted an answer to. "How's Natalie? Did she get all settled in?"

"She calls occasionally," Lorraine said. "She left for a family reunion about two months ago, and we haven't seen her since. I'm not even sure if she's still in town." She smiled sadly. "She wanted to take Abby with her to meet Tess's family. I think one of our suspicions rang true on that one. She was here to check up on Abby and see what I'd let her get away with. Then suddenly she was gone, leaving me to explain things."

"I'm sorry. How's Abby taking it?"

"She's a kid. She'll be okay." Lorraine looked up at her and grinned. "Abby has missed you. When she got an *A* in math on her report card, she wanted to call and tell you, but she couldn't get through, or maybe you don't have the same phone number anymore."

"I've been out of town a lot lately. My messages tend to pile up after a while."

They heard Abby squeal on the other side of the restaurant, and they both looked to see what she'd won.

180

"They probably just spent six bucks trying to get a thirty-five-cent bear," Lorraine said with a chuckle. She crossed her arms over her chest in a familiar pose that Dorian had nearly forgotten. "I've been in therapy for about six weeks now," Lorraine said, "and it's really helped." She searched Dorian's face. "You made me realize that I had unfinished business with Tess. I'd never taken the time to really grieve for her. After she died I had a baby to take care of. I'm learning how to deal with it and let go of a few things. I've learned a lot about myself and how Tess's death has shaped our lives." She smiled again. "I'm a slow learner sometimes."

"I'm glad it's all starting to come together for you."

Lorraine took a deep breath. "One of the things in my life that I truly regret, Dorian, is hurting you. If I had that to do over again —"

Abby came back to the table with an armload of stuffed toys. "Look what we won!"

"Wow," Lorraine said. "Quite a haul." As Mia slid into the booth, Lorraine said, "What did these cost you? About thirty bucks?"

"Eight," Mia replied with a laugh. "And worth every cent." She opened her menu. "Let's eat. Spending money always makes me hungry."

Out in the parking lot a while later, Dorian gave Abby a hug and didn't want to let go of her.

"When are you coming over to see me on my skates?"

Dorian tousled Abby's hair and laughed. "You got skates?"

Mia looked at Lorraine and said, "I thought she only did that with me, that instead-of-answering-your-question-I'll-ask-you-one-of-my-own thing."

"Oh no," Lorraine said with a grin. "She does that with everybody." She gave Dorian a long hug and quietly said, "Don't be a stranger, okay? We miss you." When she let go of her, Dorian could see tears welling up in Lorraine's eyes.

"Okay."

"It was nice meeting you, Mia," Lorraine said. She helped Abby get the stuffed animals in the back seat and waved as Mia and Dorian went off in the direction of Dorian's Jeep.

"Now do you believe me?" Mia said as they drove out of the parking lot. "She's more than crazy about you. I think she's in love with you."

"She was crying when we left," Dorian said. Even through her surprise and confusion, things were starting to register. *Lorraine was crying . . .*

"What did she say to you?" Mia asked.

Dorian shrugged and looked over at her.

Mia threw her hands up in the air. "Clueless. You really *are* clueless. Did you two talk at all while Abby and I fished toys out of that machine?"

"She said she was sorry about what happened. Jesus, Mia. Do you really think —?"

"There's only one way to find out. Take me home and then go over and see her."

* * * * *

Dorian drove around the block twice as she tried to decide whether or not it would be best to call first. The third time around, however, she just parked in the driveway and got out of the Jeep before she changed her mind.

Lorraine answered the door and then leaned against it with her eyes closed for just a moment. "God, it's good to have you here," she whispered. "Come in. Please. We were just talking about you."

"Dorian!" Abby said as she bounced off the sofa. "Can I show her my skates, Rainey? Can I?"

"Maybe later," Lorraine said. "I thought we were putting a puzzle together. I like the apple orchard one. It's always a challenge." She sent Abby off to a hall closet to find the puzzle and then offered Dorian something to drink. "What brings you to our humble abode?" she asked as she sat down next to her on the sofa. "On second thought, it doesn't matter why you're here." Lorraine reached over and touched Dorian's hand. "God, I've missed you."

"I've missed you too," Dorian said, her voice full of emotion. "More than you know."

"Then tell me about it." Lorraine's hand moved to the back of Dorian's neck where she slowly played with the hair near the top of her collar. "Tell me," she whispered.

"I want to stay here tonight. I need to be with you."

Lorraine pulled her closer and whispered, "I want that too." She kissed her, and that warm, safe feeling slowly spread through Dorian's veins and her head began to swim from the fluttering in her stomach.

Love had such an interesting way of expressing itself in her body.

Lorraine's kiss moved to Dorian's neck and throat, and Dorian chuckled when she heard Lorraine whisper, "You know what? You really *do* smell good."

About the Author

Peggy J. Herring lives on seven acres of mesquite in south Texas with her cockatiel, hermit crabs and two wooden cats. When she isn't writing, Peggy enjoys fishing and traveling. She is the author of *Love's Harvest*, *Hot Check*, *Those Who Wait* from Naiad Press and *White Lace and Promises*, *Calm Before the Storm*, *The Comfort of Strangers* and *Beyond All Reason* from Bella Books. In addition, Peggy has contributed short stories to several Naiad anthologies, including *The First Time Ever*, *Dancing In the Dark*, *Lady Be Good*, *The Touch of Your Hand*, and *The Very Thought of You*. Peggy is currently working on a new romance titled *Midnight Rain* to be released by Bella Books in 2005.

Publications from
BELLA BOOKS, INC.
The best in contemporary lesbian fiction

P.O. Box 10543, Tallahassee, FL 32302
Phone: 800-729-4992
www.bellabooks.com

TALK OF THE TOWN TOO by Saxon Bennett. 181 pp. Second in the series about wild and fun loving friends. ISBN 1-931513-77-5 $12.95

LOVE SPEAKS HER NAME by Laura DeHart Young. 170 pp. Love and friendship, desire and intrigue, spark this exciting sequel to *Forever and the Night.*
ISBN 1-59493-002-3 $12.95

TO HAVE AND TO HOLD by Peggy J. Herring. 184 pp. By finally letting down her defenses, will Dorian be opening herself to a devastating betrayal?
ISBN 1-59493-005-8 $12.95

WILD THINGS by Karin Kallmaker. 228 pp. Dutiful daughter Faith has met the perfect man. There's just one problem: she's in love with his sister. ISBN 1-931513-64-3 $12.95

SHARED WINDS by Kenna White. 216 pp. Can Emma rebuild more than just Lanny's marina? ISBN 1-59493-006-6 $12.95

THE UNKNOWN MILE by Jaime Clevenger. 253 pp. Kelly's world is getting more and more complicated every moment. ISBN 1-931513-57-0 $12.95

TREASURED PAST by Linda Hill. 189 pp. A shared passion for antiques leads to love.
ISBN 1-59493-003-1 $12.95

SIERRA CITY by Gerri Hill. 284 pp. Chris and Jesse cannot deny their growing attraction . . . ISBN 1-931513-98-8 $12.95

ALL THE WRONG PLACES by Karin Kallmaker. 174 pp. Sex and the single girl—Brandy is looking for love and usually she finds it. Karin Kallmaker's first *After Dark* erotic novel. ISBN 1-931513-76-7 $12.95

WHEN THE CORPSE LIES A Motor City Thriller by Therese Szymanski. 328 pp. Butch bad-girl Brett Higgins is used to waking up next to beautiful women she hardly knows. Problem is, this one's dead. ISBN 1-931513-74-0 $12.95

GUARDED HEARTS by Hannah Rickard. 240 pp. Someone's reminding Alyssa about her secret past, and then she becomes the suspect in a series of burglaries.
ISBN 1-931513-99-6 $12.95

ONCE MORE WITH FEELING by Peggy J. Herring. 184 pp. Lighthearted, loving, romantic adventure. ISBN 1-931513-60-0 $12.95